OUTRAG

Lauren and Sandy's h
you make it down you
real careful in there. Go right at the
take the dirt road till you get to the taco stand. You'll find a phone there.'

Sandy groaned. 'I might have known it wouldn't just be a block and a half to the corner store . . .' She turned to Lauren. 'How did that bit from *Hamlet* go again?' she asked.

'To suffer the slings and arrows of outrageous fortune.'

'Yeah, that . . . poor guy – I know just how he felt . . .'

OUTRAGEOUS FORTUNE

A Novel by Robin Turner
Based on the Motion Picture from Touchstone Pictures
Produced by Ted Field, Robert W. Cort
Based on the Motion Picture written by Leslie Dixon
Directed by Arthur Hiller

A STAR BOOK
published by
the Paperback Division of
W.H. ALLEN & Co. PLC

A Star Book
Published in 1987
by the Paperback Division of
W.H. Allen & Co. Plc
44 Hill Street, London W1X 8LB

Printed and bound in Great Britain by
Anchor Brendon Ltd, Tiptree, Essex

ISBN 0 352 32080 X

Chapter One

The New York Institute of Dramatic Art is one of the world's greatest theatrical institutions. Every day, hundreds of dedicated students brave the weirdos on the New York Subway just for the opportunity of being able to study with some of the acknowledged masters of the performing arts.

Shakespeare, Strindberg, Brecht – all the greats and some of the not-so-greats are studied here. In addition there are dance classes, music classes, mime classes, awareness classes – everything, in short, to prepare a person for a successful career in the American theatre, and maybe even stardom.

It's unfortunate then that the acting profession is so hopelessly overcrowded. Most students just don't make it and give up their struggle, sacrificing their craft to become teachers, accountants, or waiters in *Joe Allen's*. With so few theatres around these days many would-be actors and actresses never even get the chance to perform in front of a live audience, let alone make a living out of acting.

Luck plays a large part in it. Many actors with a minimum of talent but a maximum of more physical attributes make the big time and go on to Broadway or Hollywood. Other immensely gifted actors spend the rest of their lives performing in cold empty halls to uninterested audiences.

And for others, the big chance is waiting just around the corner...

In a cold and roomy rehearsal studio at the Institute the air shrilled to the sound of metal upon metal, foil upon foil. A fencing class was in full swing. Pairs of masked white-clad fencers were going through the practised motions of classical fencing – the parry, the thrust and the riposte. Their teacher, a Douglas Fairbanks look-alike, watched from his vantage point of a small raised platform. To him the pairs of fencers formed a picture of studied grace, poise and elegance.

All, that is, except one.

These two were going at it like a pair of manic musketeers, thrashing furiously at each other in an apparent attempt to be the first one to draw blood. They grunted and cursed, backed away and then attacked once more. This was not *The Prisoner of Zenda*, their teacher reflected wryly; this was getting uncomfortably close to *The Texas Chainsaw Massacre.*

Finally the fencer who had been getting the worst of it retreated and indicated that her rival should stop her one-woman course of savagery and destruction. She took off her mask and called up to her teacher: 'Would you tell her to stop! She's trying to kill me!'

'Isn't that the idea?' asked her partner in all innocence. She also took off her mask to reveal a round, attractive, refined face framed with locks of honey-blonde hair.

'No, Lauren,' the teacher said patiently, coming over to her. 'This is *theatrical* fencing, not an autopsy...

Right?'

'All right...' agreed Lauren, genuinely sorry and embarrassed. That had always been her trouble – she always got so involved in a part. But then, wasn't that what good acting was all about? Hadn't the great Stanislavsky said...?

'I don't even know why they make us do this,' complained her opponent after Douglas Fairbanks had walked away.

'You want to do Shakespeare, don't you?' Lauren asked in her precise tones. Her partner nodded, and Lauren continued: 'Well, Shakespearean people have duels.'

'Not the women,' her friend reminded her.

Lauren put on her best *grande dame de théâtre* voice. 'It happens to be my ambition to play Hamlet,' she declared loftily, and stalked off with a Bette Davis toss of her hair.

Behind her, her partner made signals to her fellow students about Lauren's current state of mental health.

'That'll pack 'em in the aisles,' she said sarcastically and went off to nurse her bruises.

Whatever grace Lauren might have lacked in her fencing class she more than made up for in ballet class. Lauren was a natural dancer, tall, long-legged, lithe and athletic. The dance teacher was putting his students through their routines and making them practise their *jetés*. As each student finished his or her leap, he would make a tiny chalk mark on the floor to indicate where they had landed. A long-legged black girl had just completed a near faultless jump of about ten feet and now it was Lauren's turn.

Lauren walked to the front of the line, her eyes fixed

firmly ahead and her brow furrowed in concentration. She took a few long deep breaths and then leapt, sailing effortlessly through the air, landing almost three feet past the other girl's mark.

'Bitch,' said the black girl as Lauren bounced past her, grinning smugly, and made her way to the ballet barre.

After she had been limbering up for a few minutes, a firm hand touched her shoulder.

'Lauren,' said a husky voice. Lauren turned around. The voice belonged to one of her fellow dancers, a blond-haired, blue-eyed, all-American boy.

'Hi, George,' Lauren said indifferently.

George leant over her, looking deep into her eyes. 'Have dinner with me tonight,' he said seductively.

Lauren did an instant double take. 'What?'

'Say yes,' George persisted.

'George,' demanded Lauren, standing up and placing a hand on her hip. 'Why are you acting like this?'

'Because I want to be with you . . .' he smouldered. His tone was honeyed, seductive, totally irresistible.

'Well, that's really, *really* nice,' she said, touched and even a little aroused by George's amorous advances. Suddenly she fell into a helpless giggle. 'This is so funny – I mean, I always thought you were gay . . .'

George looked hurt. 'Well, I am . . . But I play so many heterosexual roles I really feel I need to do some serious research.'

Lauren sighed in horror, raising her eyes heavenwards. Were there no depths to which an actor wouldn't sink? One day, she promised herself, one day I'm going to get a starring role *and* meet a man who's kind, generous, good-looking, single and totally and irretrievably *straight*.

All she needed was a little good fortune and, knowing the New York theatre, a lot of divine intervention . . .

Chapter Two

Lauren's blue eyes gaped even wider as she read the hand-written card which had been pinned to the students' noticeboard:

Winter Class Now Open
Stanislav Korzenowski
By Audition Only

Stanislav Korzenowski, the great dramatic coach and inheritor of the mantle of Stanislavsky, producer of some of the most critically acclaimed Broadway successes of the past twenty years, was going to lecture at the Institute! Dreamy-eyed, Lauren turned to a friend. 'Korzenowski.' She repeated the name almost reverentially. 'Can you believe it? I have got to get into that class. He is just the greatest –'

'Yeah,' interrupted her companion, a notoriously down-to-earth New Yorker. 'But where are you gonna get that sort of money?'

Lauren's face fell. Short of sticking up the Chase Manhattan Bank or holding Nancy Reagan hostage, there was only one way . . .

*

It probably would be easier kidnapping Nancy Reagan, reflected Lauren as she pressed the buzzer labelled *Ames* at the entrance to her parent's uptown apartment building. As she considered the possibilities of breaking into the White House, she stepped slightly to one side, trying to avoid the probing eye of the video camera above the door.

'Who is it?' demanded the strident voice at the other end of the intercom.

Still keeping out of the camera's line of vision, Lauren affected her best Brooklyn accent: 'It's yuh sister-in-law! Hurry up! My feet're fallin' off!'

Lauren's mother's voice immediately softened. 'Well, hi, Shir –' She stopped, suddenly suspicious. 'Wait a minute – get in front of the camera.'

Lauren sighed. It was a nice try, but she should have known it would have been easier fooling White House Security.

She stepped in front of the camera and smiled her sweetest little girl smile, hoping that it might at least warm her mother's stony heart.

It didn't.

'No. We can't afford it,' her mother's voice cracked through the entryphone as she recognised her only daughter.

Lauren stamped her foot in frustration. 'Come on, Mom,' she pleaded. 'Let me in, please . . .'

'Is that my baby?' asked a male voice on the phone.

'Yes, but she can't come in,' Mrs Ames replied. 'She wants a loan.'

Lauren's face brightened as she recognised her father's voice and she looked up adorably at the camera. 'Daddy, can't I please come in? Please, Daddy . . .'

The opening mechanism on the door buzzed into life,

but was cut short before Lauren could open the door. She could hear her parents' voices arguing on the intercom:

'Warren, what are you doing?'

'You don't *know* she wants money!'

'Yeah, Mom,' Lauren spoke into the phone. 'Can't I just drop by and see my parents?'

Her effort to sound like the dutiful daughter was greeted by an icy silence. Admitting defeat, Lauren took a deep breath: 'All right I need a five thousand dollar loan but it is to study with Korzenowski and I'll pay you back just as soon as I –'

'*What did you say? What was that?*' demanded her mother.

Lauren sighed, and wondered how quickly the President would pay up on Mrs Reagan. She felt just like Jackie Coogan in *Oliver Twist* asking for some more.

'I know I owe you some money . . .' she admitted.

'Thirty-five thousand dollars and fifty-nine cents, to be exact,' her mother reminded her.

'But it's *the* Korzenowski!'

'And before that it was Yale and RADA and the Institute.' Her mother's voice took on a gentle tone. 'Lauren, you've been at this acting thing for years and you still haven't earned a penny. You're still working as a salesgirl . . . Honey, face it, maybe it's time to give up . . .'

Lauren's face fell once more. Maybe her mother was right, maybe she didn't have what it took to be an actress . . . She brushed a lone tear from her cheek and was about to say something when a piece of paper fluttered down from the sky and landed at her feet. She picked it up. It was a cheque made out to Lauren Ames for five thousand dollars. She read it excitedly and then looked up at the open window of her parents' first-floor apartment. Her father was standing there, smiling at his little girl's obvious joy.

'Thank you, Daddy!' cried Lauren and blew him a heartfelt kiss. She skipped off down the street. At last she was going to study with the great Korzenowski and become a *real* actress.

'Here's my application – *and* my down-payment,' Lauren said, handing a cheque to the frosty-faced woman behind the desk.

The receptionist looked up icily at Lauren's eager face and handed her back the cheque. 'Keep that for now,' she said. 'You still have to audition for Mister Korzenowski.' She indicated a row of red plastic chairs to the left. 'Please sit down there. Mister Korzenowski will call you when he is ready.'

Lauren went over to join the group of fellow students, all of whom looked extremely apprehensive as they silently rehearsed their audition pieces and composed themselves for the coming ordeal. She sat down next to a pleasant-faced, slightly whimpish young man in glasses.

'Are you nervous?' he asked her suddenly, making her jump. She darted him a look which would have annihilated Bette Davis at twenty paces.

'Sorry... I'm *really* sorry,' he apologised with practised sincerity. 'I guess we're all a little...' He caught Lauren's menacing glare. 'Don't talk, right? I don't blame you... this is so intense... sorry... Shut up, Weldon. Sorry... sorry...'

Finally Weldon made good his promise and shut up. He returned to studying his left shoe.

Lauren sat back and put her hands to her temples, attempting to ease away the tension before the coming audition.

Suddenly the door to the waiting room burst open and into the room blasted something which could be best described as a cross between Phyllis Diller, Madonna and Tina Turner on speed. The general effect on the students was roughly akin to that of a four minute warning: confusion and total disorientation.

The newcomer was dressed in tight leather trousers and boots, and a leopard skin shirt which covered up very little of her amply endowed chest. Her fingers which ended in long blood-red finger nails were adorned with cheap gaudy rings and around her neck she wore a chain which looked as though it had begun life in a public lavatory. Her hair, which had a life all of its own, was fiery red and frizzed out in all directions.

The newcomer gallumphed over to the stony-faced receptionist and in a voice which was the end product of sixty Marlboros and several whiskies a day asked: 'You got a phone I can use?'

The receptionist, seemingly unphased by this magnificent bundle of sleaze and trash, indicated the phone on her desk. The newcomer took a red card out of her zebra skin shoulder bag, picked up the receiver and dialled.

'Hi, this is Sandy Brozinsky,' she said to the voice at the other end of the line. 'What's your name? Howie? OK, Howie, I am holding in my hand this little thingie which says you're gonna turn my phone off at noon.'

The students listened on, fascinated, as Sandy continued her spiel with the clerk at the phone company. Some of them noticed that the clock on the wall read three minutes to twelve.

'Yeah, well I wanna tell you something,' Sandy said to Howie. 'I've just got home after two months' intensive care. They *wheel* me into my building and what do I find when I open the mailbox but your little thingie saying that I have until noon today... No, you listen!' she barked in to the receiver as the beleagured Howie tried to get a word in edgeways. 'I just opened the damn thing, I have just now laid eyes on it for the first time... What was I supposed to do, have them unhook my life support system so I could pay the bills?' Sandy paused, more in order to catch her breath than to let Howie speak. 'OK, so now I have three – no, two – minutes to write a cheque and *wheel* myself down to your office. Is that the drill, Howie?'

Howie, by now totally intimidated, mumbled a few hesitant words down the phone. Sandy broke out into a large, and not unattractive, smile. 'Twenty-four hours? Twenty-four big ones,' she said gratefully. 'You're a prince among men, Howie, I mean it. I want to have your child... Yeah goodbye.'

Sandy put the phone down and rubbed her hands together triumphantly. 'Right! Now who's got a cigarette?' she asked.

Lauren came out of her state of shock to realise that the screaming, lying, red-haired banshee was addressing her.

'*I* don't smoke,' she said self-righteously.

Before Lauren had the chance to quote the Surgeon General's latest statistics, Sandy turned and stole one from the receptionist's pack who was too busy at her typewriter to notice. Picking up the phone again she started to dial another number.

It was then that Lauren decided to stand up for herself and her fellow students. 'Excuse me,' she started with quiet dignity, 'would you *please* not screech at anyone else right now? I'm preparing for an audition.'

Sandy put the phone down. She was really interested. 'Yeah? For what?'

'A workshop with Stanislav Korzenowski,' Lauren replied smugly.

'Who's that?'

'Only one of the greatest theatrical geniuses in the world,' Lauren explained patiently. 'Now, if you don't mind . . .'

'Hey, maybe I should audition for that,' Sandy said. 'I'm an actress.' In response to everyone's look of disbelief she added, 'Hey no, I'm a pro.'

Lauren snorted with contempt.

'I'm more of a pro than you are,' Sandy retaliated.

'I sincerely doubt that.' Who was this two-bit . . . tart . . . trying to fool?

Sandy took the offensive: 'OK – what have you done?'

'Most recently?' Lauren asked relishing the opportunity of putting down this self-assured newcomer. 'I've played Cordelia, Miranda, Beatrice, Antigone . . .' She reeled off a list of the very best classical roles, none of which meant anything to Sandy. 'Before that I was in the off-off-Broadway production of *The Potato Famine* – I was First Apparition.'

'Apparition?' Sandy was not impressed.

'Yes,' said Lauren proudly. 'I was in the vision that they saw in the end when they all starved to death . . .'

'I missed that one.' There was sarcasm in Sandy's voice.

'It was a good little musical.'

Sandy shrugged. Irish famine victims were, she supposed, a natural progression from mangy alley cats and South American dictators' wives. Determined not to be upstaged by any Apparition, First or not, she asked: 'You make much money outta these plays?'

Lauren's aloof silence provided the answer.

'Well . . . I just made twenty-five hundred bucks doing

a movie,' bragged Sandy.

'That's where I've seen you before!' Weldon suddenly piped up. 'In the movies!'

'*You* saw *Ninja Vixens*?'

'I... uh, I guess I must have...' he muttered and immediately shut up again.

'This whole acting thing's goin' pretty good,' continued Sandy, delighted at everyone's stares of appreciation. 'I mean, it's all just bullshitting, right! Actors are just bullshitters who get paid... Now, where do I sign up?' she asked the frosty receptionist who handed her an application form.

This was simply too much for Lauren. Not only had this walking, talking trash can disturbed her pre-audition exercises, *and* derided and debased the sacred vocation of the theatre, now she was going to sign up for what she apparently thought to be nothing more than a course of organised bullshitting. It was time for Lauren to stand up for the theatrical tradition, for Ellen Terry, La Duse and Sarah Bernhardt, and all those past masters who even now must be turning in their graves.

'Just exactly what do you think you're going to do in there?' she asked.

Sandy shrugged. 'I dunno... I'll make something up...'

Lauren couldn't believe her ears. 'You're planning to audition for Korzenowski and wing it?'

'Jesus, you'd think I was gonna pee on him!'

Lauren took her aside as one might an inexperienced child. 'Now, listen to me,' she began condescendingly. 'You don't audition for a man of Korzenowski's stature without a prepared *classical* monologue...' Sandy stared blankly at her as she continued. 'That means Shaw, Ibsen, Shakespeare,' she said, hoping that Sandy would at least recognise those names. '*I* am doing Ophelia's mad scene... I am not waltzing in off the street saying "Hey, I want to be an actress".'

Sandy seemed suitably cowed for a moment and then carefully looked Lauren up and down, before saying in her most matter-of-fact voice: 'You know what, I bet you haven't been laid in about a year...'

Lauren gasped, for once speechless. Fuming with rage she tried to come up with a reply when a dark threatening voice announced in an East European accent: 'Ames, Lauren!'

Lauren turned. Standing in the doorway, like a figure out of Hollywood's worst nightmare, was a small balding man with a stern disdainful face. He was dressed in riding breeches and long black boots. He wore a monocle in his right eye. In one hand he held a director's baton; the other beckoned Lauren towards him.

Like Helen Chandler accepting Bela Lugosi's offer of a quick bite, Lauren slowly followed the great director into the audition room.

As she passed by, Sandy called sweetly after her: 'Have a good mad scene...'

Chapter Three

Late that night in his office, Korzenowski sat alone at his desk, carefully sifting through the photographs and résumés of all the candidates who had attended the audition. Most of the photographs he would toss mercilessly into the waste paper bin, but occasionally he would stop, take a thoughtful sip of brandy and study one more closely.

After an hour only about ten résumés remained on his desk. He was particularly drawn to the photos of Lauren and Sandy. He looked slowly at one and then the other, then referred back to their résumés.

A smile cracked his otherwise threatening features and he began to chuckle evilly to himself.

It was a chuckle Peter Lorre would have been proud of . . .

Lauren could hardly believe her good fortune: here she was, finally accepted as a member of Korzenowski's class, picked out from hundreds of young hopefuls. At last she would be able to prove to her parents that all their sacrifices had been worth every penny. She felt totally vindicated; and very, very proud.

She looked around, recognising some faces, and sharing in their obvious joy. Weldon had made the class too. There was, of course, no sign of Sandy.

As the great man himself entered the classroom, Weldon began to fidget nervously. Lauren didn't mind: in spite of their rather fraught first meeting she sort of liked him. He was cute – in a dorkish kind of way.

Korzenowski strode purposefully to the front of the class and turned to address his students.

'I will wish you to keep notes of everything I say – I will also wish to look at those notes,' he began sternly. 'If you say this is like school I make no apologies . . .' His voice suddenly softened and there was a twinkle in his eyes. 'I am an old egotist and I want to know that you record my ideas.'

A gentle murmur of appreciative laughter buzzed around the classroom before his voice once more turned to ice: 'If you do not, you are gone from this class.'

Ten instantly terrified students began to take down the great man's every word.

'We begin with vowel groups. There are over four hundred . . . Unless you can recognise each and every one you will never be able to do dialects, never be able to talk like an English duchess or a Brooklyn cop . . .'

The door suddenly crashed open to reveal Sandy standing there, her face flushed and her hair even wilder than usual.

'Sorry I'm late,' she said in response to Korzenowski's look of disapproval. 'They made me fill out all those dumb-ass financial aid forms.'

Her mouth agape with disbelief Lauren tried to convince herself that this wasn't really happening.

The following day Lauren still hadn't got over the fact

that Sandy had been accepted into Korzenowski's class.

'I mean, I absolutely cannot believe that he let *her* in *and* on a scholarship,' she said to her colleague in the theatrical costumier's where she worked part-time. Her colleague nodded sympathetically; it was only the fourth time she had heard the story today.

'I bet I know what she did for an audition,' bitched Lauren. 'That – *tramp* – has no training, no experience ... I mean, correct me if I'm wrong but I thought that if you work at your craft, maybe, just possibly, you get to work with one of the greats –'

Her friend stopped her flow to point out to her the fat little kid at the counter who wanted to buy a pair of joke spectacles.

Muttering her apologies, Lauren took the spectacles and rang up the price. Her friend gently remarked: 'Lauren, that's $2.95, not $295.00 ...'

'*I know! I know!*' Lauren snapped back and then buried her face in her hands. 'Oh my God, I'm sorry. I'm really sorry. It's just that ... there's something wrong with my life ...'

'Why don't you go out the back and rest a while?' her friend suggested. 'I'll serve the kid.'

Lauren nodded and left the counter. What was happening to her? Her life was in a mess: she had no career, she was getting nowhere with her acting, she owed her parents money, she was surrounded by incompetents like Sandy Brozinsky and ... and ... and she hadn't been laid in over a year.

'Excuse me?' A hand tapped her on the shoulder. She looked around – and her eyes almost popped out of her head in amazement.

This was no ordinary-looking guy, this wasn't even your average GQ model. This was pure, uncensored, drop-dead, knock-'em-in-the-aisles, heart-breaking, I'll-follow-you-to-the-ends-of-the-earth, hunk material. This was a combination of Richard Gere, Tom Sellick, Mel Gibson and Superman. Lauren decided she'd died and gone to heaven.

'Are you feeling all right?' he asked her.

Lauren looked around, unable to believe that the hunk was actually talking to her. 'Uh, better . . .' she squeaked. 'I was just . . . who cares? Can I help you?'

The hunk looked at her coyly. 'Well, I was wondering if you had anything in pumpkin?'

'In the shade pumpkin?'

'No, a pumpkin costume,' the hunk laughed. 'I sound like an idiot, don't I? The reason is, I teach grammar school.'

Lauren did a double take. '*You're* a schoolteacher?' she asked incredulously. Mind-blowing good looks and brains as well?

The hunk smiled. It was the most dazzling smile Lauren had seen in her life. 'That's right.'

'You're *not* an actor?'

The hunk laughed again as Lauren felt her knees turn to jelly. 'God, no, I'd be terrible,' he said with endearing modesty. 'What made you think that?'

'So many actors come into this store I just thought . . .' Lauren flustered and then checked herself. Play it cool, keep control of yourself, she told herself. This is too good to be true – mind-blowing good looks, brains, modesty *and he's not an actor*! She tried to control her quavering voice. 'Never mind . . . go on . . .'

'Well, we're doing this school pageant. There's this little kid who's very insecure. The other kids pick on him. His mother doesn't sew and I just thought it'd give him a real big boost to have the best costume in the whole place.' The hunk flushed with embarrassment and continued: 'So I thought a professional costumier's would have an incredible pumpkin... I couldn't go more than fifty bucks because this is out of my own pocket...'

Lauren almost swooned. Not only was he gorgeous, intelligent, modest, sensitive, *normal* – he also happened to be Jimmy Stewart.

'I really am sorry... I don't think we have a pumpkin.'

His face fell. 'Oh... Then what about a squash?' he asked hopefully.

Lauren hated to disappoint him again. 'We don't have any vegetables as such,' she said. 'I'm really sorry.' She meant it.

The hunk looked crestfallen, like a disappointed kid. It made him look even cuter; Lauren wanted to take him in her arms and cuddle him. 'Well, this was the last place in the list,' he said. 'Don't worry – I'll throw something together.'

As he turned to go he gave Lauren one last look with those deep, deep blue eyes. Lauren swallowed hard. There were only a certain number of things a grown woman could be expected to take...

'Listen... maybe someone, maybe I...' she stuttered at a loss for words but knowing that there was no way she was going to let this gorgeous hunk out of her life. If she did she'd never be able to look herself in the face again. 'I've... uh, I've made a lot of my own costumes... it probably wouldn't be that difficult... I mean, if I can help in any way at all...'

Chapter Four

Lauren smiled contentedly as she gazed dreamily into the hunk's deep, deep blue eyes. His bare muscular arms enfolded her completely, as she snuggled closer to him, bringing her head to settle down onto his full broad chest.

The state of Lauren's bed and the sweat still glistening on their bodies bore silent testimony of their love-making. To one side of the bed lay the unfinished pumpkin costume; the poor little kid would just have to wait for his surprise. For the moment all Lauren could think about was the way Michael had taken her in his arms and made love to her the way she thought no man ever could. When it came to men like him, Shakespeare and pumpkin costumes didn't stand a chance.

'Lauren, I really hope you'll forgive me,' said Michael. 'I don't usually lunge at women . . . you just . . . I don't know, I just had to kiss you . . . I'm sorry. I really hope you'll want to see me again.'

Lauren burst out laughing. She couldn't believe it. Here was this gorgeous man who half the women in the world would gladly die for, here was this fabulous guy in *her* bed, apologising for sweeping her off her feet! Not for the first time today she had to tell herself that this wasn't a dream, that this was really happening.

'Michael, where in the world do you come from?' she asked. If he'd had said Mount Olympus she wouldn't have been at all surprised.

'New Mexico originally,' he said seriously.

'No, I mean, how can a delightful man like you just be wandering the streets of New York?' Struck by a sudden doubt she grabbed his left hand and looked at the third finger. 'And single!' she grinned. 'I just can't believe it!'

Michael looked sheepish. 'Well, that's not really out of choice... I'd like to get married.'

'This isn't happening,' Lauren marvelled.

Michael chuckled. 'Why not?'

'Come on,' Lauren said, 'There's got to be something wrong with you? What are your faults?'

Michael thought about this for a moment before replying: 'I smoke.'

'That's it? You smoke?'

'Nonono, it's terrible. I'm an addict.' Michael smiled and reached over to his jacket which hung on a bedside chair. He took out a small pouch of tobacco from the pocket. 'Colton's tobacco – New Mexico's finest.' He looked concerned. 'I hope you don't mind.'

'I'll struggle through somehow,' she said, pretending to put a brave face on it, but only succeeding in breaking into yet another wide grin.

Michael grinned back, displaying his perfect white teeth. 'I'm glad because... now, I don't want to push you or anything but... could I see you tomorrow night?'

Lauren nodded, looking into his deep, deep blue eyes tenderly, seductively. As he drew her nearer to kiss her, Lauren suddenly realised that for the past twenty-six years she had been living under a terrible misconception.

There really was a Santa Claus after all.

Later that night Lauren was sitting at her sewing machine, putting the finishing touches to the pumpkin costume. By her side, Michael was smoking a roll-up of Colton's and idly flicking through the pages of Lauren's notebook.

'Is this what you learn in acting class?' he asked, indicating a page. 'What the heck are these?'

'Vowel groups,' replied Lauren as she put down her costume and heaved a sigh of relief at finally finishing.

Michael flung down the notebook and took her possessively in his arms. Gently he led her back into the bedroom.

The following morning Lauren was blissfully unaware of the mayhem of rush hour New York as she waited by the only store in Manhattan which stocked Michael's brand of tobacco. In fact, even if they had gone and dropped a nuclear warhead right in the middle of Broadway, Lauren was so out of it that she wouldn't have even blinked.

Michael came out and took her hand. Together they walked down to Greenwich Village, whispering tender endearments to each other. Passers-by who stopped to stare winked knowingly at each other: here was a young couple obviously very much in love.

Michael accompanied Lauren to the doors of the Institute and then kissed her goodbye. It was a long, lingering, passionate kiss. Dreamy-eyed, Lauren watched him walk away and then made her way off to class.

As she entered the classroom, Sandy turned round. Lauren's euphoric smile and the way she walked slightly bow-legged told her all she needed to know.

'That kind of evening, huh?' she bitched loudly across the classroom.

Lauren floated on by smugly. 'Not the kind you're used to,' she countered expertly. 'No money changed hands.'

'There are more important things than words,' Korzenowski announced to his class. All of them were dilligently taking notes. 'Today we are going to work *without* words. All right, Eddie – reveal!'

Eddie, a young black student, stood up uncertainly and walked to the front of the class. After a few moments' hesitation he suddenly cried out: 'AKA AKKAWANMNA-GAH!'

It was a brilliant imitation of a chicken being slowly strangled.

Korzenowski regarded Eddie's barnyard impression with disgust. 'No, no. Reveal!' he barked. 'You have killed your father, married your mother! What are you feeling? No words!'

Eddie screwed up his eyes in concentration and let loose a bizarre howl. When he had finished, he looked expectantly around for approval.

'What we have here,' said the master, 'is a sick sea lion.' He waved the dejected Eddie back to his seat and turned on Sandy. There was a malicious glint in his eyes. 'Now, Miss Brozinsky, you will do – also without words – Hamlet's soliloquy.'

Sandy stood up nervously. 'Hamlet – that's Shakespeare, right?'

Korzenowski raised his eyes heavenwards in mock horror. 'Is it possible that you have never read the tragedy of Hamlet?' he enquired sarcastically.

'Well, sure – in high school,' retorted Sandy, suddenly on the defensive. 'Look, I gotta tell you, I never could get through it.'

Korzenowski regarded her with all the respect he would accord to a dead flea. He turned to the rest of the class, completely ignoring Sandy. 'Well, then – we will have to give her the comic book,' he said acidly.

The class burst into laughter, a welcome release from the tension which had been building up.

Totally humiliated, Sandy looked daggers at her teacher. If looks could kill they would soon be buying flowers for Korzenowski's funeral.

Seething with fury and muttering angrily to herself, Sandy fumbled in her bag for the keys to her apartment. Before she could find them, the door was snatched open and standing before her was Michael, all six gorgeous feet of him.

'Hi, Baby,' she said, planting a passionate kiss on his lips. 'That bastard' – she kissed him again – 'damn class is driving me . . . mmmm . . .'

As she came up for air, she felt that something was wrong. She looked into Michael's deep, deep blue eyes: they seemed worried, distracted.

'What's wrong, baby?' she asked with real concern. He was just about to say something when a wicked smile lit up Sandy's face. 'Not a word,' she said. 'I know *exactly* what you need.'

With a whoop of delight she pushed him back into the apartment and slammed shut the door behind them.

Chapter Five

'Death!' Korzenowski pronounced the word with obvious relish, sounding like Boris Karloff on one of his nastier days. The class responded to the word like a bunch of Transylvanian peasants who have just heard that the old master has returned to the local castle.

'Death!' he repeated. 'To die on stage is perhaps the single greatest challenge an actor must face. The audience must believe – must know – that the very life is going out of your body. Now, you!' He pointed at Weldon who nervously stepped forward. This was the moment he had been dreading.

Korzenowski strode up to him and put both his hands around Weldon's throat. 'You will die now, please,' he said. Slowly he began to squeeze at Weldon's throat. Weldon gasped and began to turn blue.

'I don't believe you,' snarled Korzenowski. 'Maintain your concentration!' His eyes gleamed with murderous intent, as he increased the pressure on Weldon's neck. Weldon's eyes bulged. His impersonation of a strangler's victim was rapidly becoming reality.

'I don't believe you!' cried Korzenowski. 'Maintain your focus!'

Weldon's eyes glazed over and he bagan to fall to the floor. Lauren leapt out of her seat, dashed over and began to tug at Korzenowski's fingers. 'Stop it!' she screamed.

Eventually she managed to prise Korzenowski's fingers away from Weldon's neck. She bent anxiously over him: he lay on the floor semi-conscious.

'Weldon, are you okay?'

Weldon nodded, still gasping for breath. Turning from him, she looked up suspiciously at Korzenowski. She knew Weldon wasn't acting. So, what was Korzenowski's game?

Korzenowski stood over them, flaunting his superiority. He returned Lauren's accusing stare with a glacial look.

Knowing when she was beaten, Lauren turned back to Weldon and helped him to his feet. 'He . . . he was in the moment,' she explained weakly to the rest of the class.

Weldon staggered back to his seat. Lauren was about to follow when Korzenowski called her back.

'Perhaps you would like to die now, Miss Ames?'

Lauren gulped. 'Aren't you out of time?' she asked hopefully.

'You, I think, will be shot,' continued the master. 'You will be struck by the bullet, you will lose muscle control; you will fall down dead - now.'

Lauren flinched, expecting him to produce a gun. Instead he held up his thumb and forefinger and pointed them at her.

'Bang.'

With a ladylike murmur, Lauren closed her eyes and dropped gracefully to the floor.

Korzenowski stood over her again. 'That can only be the result of years of training,' he declared emotionlessly.

At his feet, Lauren opened her eyes and looked up, grateful for the compliment. But Korzenowski hadn't finished with her yet.

'No other way would we see so false a performance, so mechanical, so thought out, never for one moment truly felt.'

Lauren was devastated. Korzenowski helped her to her feet as he continued: 'You must reach inside yourself, must move beyond the security of what you know. We know you can play Camille – but can you be a person of flesh and blood – a bank teller, a waitress . . . a *whore*?'

Lauren looked decidedly uncomfortable. Clearly the idea didn't appeal to her at all.

Korzenowski checked his watch. 'Ah, it is time. Class dismissed.'

As his pupils began to pack up and leave the room, he called after them: 'And I wish to see your notebooks. Please leave them!'

As Lauren walked the short distance from the Institute to the waiting cab her dismay and disappointment had turned to indignation and downright anger.

She opened the cab door and flung herself into the back seat: Michael was sitting there, waiting for her.

'That man is a Nazi!' she declared as they exchanged kisses. 'I have never – ever – in my life been the dumb one in my class.' They kissed again. 'And I haven't seen you in over nine hours.'

She fell into his arms as he indicated the driver to move away.

'Do you know what day it is?' he asked her. Lauren shook her head.

'It's our third week anniversary,' he replied. He leant over to the cabbie and told him to stop at the next corner.

He turned back to Lauren. 'I thought you might need some roses.'

Lauren raised a hand to protest. 'No, Michael! I know what teachers make – you can't afford any more flowers!'

It was no use. The cab stopped outside a florist's and, kissing her lightly on the cheek, Michael leapt out of the car. He waved at her and then went into the store.

Lauren sat back in her seat, ecstatically happy. There was no doubt about it, Michael was the most generous, kindest, sweetest, handsomest man she had ever known – and she was head-over-heels in love with him.

A few minutes passed. Lauren wondered what was keeping him so long. She smiled to herself: no doubt he was buying her the most elaborate bouquet he could find. Really, that man was impossible, and totally irresistible.

For the rest of her life Lauren never forgot what happened next.

She glanced over to the flower shop, expecting to see Michael emerge at any second – when, with a deafening blast, the shop window shattered outwards, sending shards of glass flying in all directions into the street. Within moments the entire shop was an inferno of flames and black acrid smoke. It was an explosion no one could ever have survived.

Lauren screamed and screamed and screamed.

Chapter Six

The Lower Levels was one of Manhattan's sleaziest and most avant-garde new wave bars. Any casual observer coming in from off the street would have been instantly reminded of the bar Harrison Ford used to frequent in *Star Wars*.

The clientele resembled a cast of extras from *The Rocky Horror Show:* girls with chalk-white faces and black lipstick, their multi-coloured hair spiked up in all directions; thin Andy Warhol look-alikes dressed all in black and carrying a copy of *Interview*; a blond-haired bodybuilder wearing a gold posing pouch and very little else. In the small dance area a spaced-out couple were dancing to the Velvet Underground. It was a scene every mother had warned her children about.

Sandy was totally in her element as she served at the bar, loading a tray with drinks and entertaining a customer with a raunchy joke. Behind her, a small portable TV was switched on, although the sound had been turned down.

'Okay, so now this bartender's really freaking out because the kangaroo is partying his butt off,' continued Sandy. 'Like, he's way out of control . . . so the bartender turns to the Polish guys and says –'

The customer, an unshaven, shabbily-dressed 1950s throwback drew Sandy's attention to the TV. On the screen a news reporter was standing in front of a blazing building. Behind her, fire engines were attempting to put out the flames while police held back the curious and ghoulish.

Indifferently, Sandy turned up the sound: *killed in the explosion were Reed Moran, the owner of the flower shop, and Michael Sanders, a teacher at Holmes Elementary School. Two terrorist groups have claimed responsibility for the blast.*

Sandy stood there in total shock. Her face was drained of all colour. Suddenly she snapped and, pushing past the others in the bar, she raced out sobbing into the street.

Chapter Seven

The New York City Morgue was a huge grey slab of a building, appropriate for its role as the final depository of so many victims of violent and senseless crimes. But Lauren was unaware of this: she had come here for one reason only – to prove to herself that Michael really was dead. She couldn't go through life without being certain. She had to see the body.

In the two short hours since the explosion Lauren had become a pale mockery of her former self. Her face was white and drawn, her eyes red and weeping. She even seemed thinner, and as she shuffled along the cold antiseptic corridors of the morgue she had to hold on to the coroner's arm for support.

'Are you sure you want to go through with this, Miss Ames?' he asked. 'We've got a positive ID from his wallet – you don't have to see him.'

'But I *want* to see him,' Lauren insisted. Her voice was cracked and hoarse.

The coroner nodded sympathetically and opened a door. The walls of the room were lined with body drawers, their occupants identified only by serial numbers. The coroner walked up to one of them and, before opening it, turned once more to Lauren.

'I warn you,' he said, 'there's very little left to see... particularly in the upper body region...'

'I *want* to see him,' she repeated with sad determination.

Reluctantly the coroner pulled out the drawer to reveal a body covered with a white sheet. 'I'm very sorry you feel a need to do this, Miss Ames...'

'Just leave me alone with him – please.'

'Very well,' he agreed and left the room.

As the door closed behind him, Lauren reached out a trembling hand to lift the sheet that covered Michael's body. Suddenly overcome with fear and apprehension she drew back. It would take her some time before she could muster the courage to take one last look at his broken and mutilated body.

She sat back in the chair and continued to stare at the covered body. In a minute she would do it – and then, and then her happy life with Michael would be over at last.

Shaking his head pitifully, the coroner walked down the corridor. As he did, he bumped into a young red-haired woman. He apologised but she didn't seem to hear – she just carried on unthinking, her red-rimmed eyes staring unblinkingly ahead. Another distraught relative of some poor bastard, he thought, and carried on his way.

By some strange instinct – maybe it was even love – Sandy knew exactly where to find Michael. As she entered the room the first thing she saw was the opened drawer revealing the sheeted body; she felt tears once again well up in her eyes.

The next thing she saw was Lauren sitting by the body.

'You!' cried Lauren. 'What are *you* doing here?'
'Me? What the fuck are *you* doing here?'

The coroner led a frail old lady dressed in black down the corridor to the morgue.

'We need you to give an ID on your husband, Mrs Goldman,' he said gently. 'I hope you don't mind...'

The old lady smiled kindly. 'I'm sure I'll be all right... and I would like to spend one last quiet moment with him...'

The coroner opened the door – to reveal a scene which could have taught Joan Collins and Linda Evans a thing or two. Tables and chairs were overturned and in the middle of the debris on the floor, going at it like a pair of demented female wrestlers, were Lauren and Sandy.

Mrs Goldman gave a shriek of horror and ran out of the room. The coroner ran after her, vainly trying to calm her shattered nerves.

Lauren and Sandy, each bloodied and bruised, had disentangled themselves from each other and had retreated to separate corners of the room where they eyed each other viciously like a pair of wild alleycats.

'Loved you?' Lauren spat out the words. '*Loved you*!'

'You're damn right he did,' Sandy screamed back.

Lauren laughed hysterically. 'That's obscene! I mean, that is an absolute obscenity!'

'No – that's reality, baby,' Sandy countered maliciously. 'Cause no way did that guy give a shit about you!'

'I don't believe that for one second he lowered himself –'

'Oh, he lowered himself all right!'

'This is all a lie,' Lauren cried. 'You're psychotic, that's what you are! I knew the first day you came into that office – you lied to the phone man, you lied your way into the class, you're lying now –'

'Lying, am I?' screeched Sandy. 'We'll see about that!'

Sandy lunged at Lauren and they resumed their battle, scratching at each other's face, clawing at each other's eyes, pulling each other's hair.

As they knocked each other brutally about, they bumped into the body on the open drawer. The sheet fell to the floor.

Lauren and Sandy instantly stopped. They stood in mute horror, staring at the body on the drawer.

It was terrible. The head and much of the upper torso was burnt and torn beyond recognition. It was hardly conceivable that this mess had once been a human being. They tried bravely to accustom themselves to the sight before them.

For a moment they stood there, shocked beyond tears and anger. Then their expressions changed as they both looked below the body's waist.

There was something odd there, something not quite right – no, something totally *wrong*. They exchanged puzzled looks.

Lauren pointed to the body's left thigh. 'There should be a birthmark there . . .' she said slowly.

'. . . and a mole. Where's the mole?'

Lauren peered more closely at the body. 'It should be next to the appendix scar . . . but . . . but . . .'

'. . . but there *is* no appendix scar!' Sandy clapped her hands in delight as she realised the wonderful implications. Forgetting their differences the girls fell joyfully into each other's arms, hopping up and down for joy.

'Son of a bitch!' cried Sandy. 'It's the wrong guy!'

'It's somebody else!' said Lauren. 'He's alive!

Michael's alive!'

The coroner wrung his hands in desperation. These two women had definitely cracked up. All around, drawers had been opened and their contents inspected as Lauren and Sandy scanned the entire dead contents of the mortuary.

Neither of them now seemed in the least bit perturbed at some of the grisly ways in which the bodies had died. All they wanted to do was to make sure that Michael had not been filed away in the wrong drawer. It was completely possible. After all, as Sandy had reminded Lauren, stranger things had happened in *Dallas*.

'For the last time, ladies,' said the coroner, his patience finally at an end. 'This is Michael Sanders. He has been identified. Now, people in your state suffer a great deal of denial –'

Lauren wagged an accusing finger at him. 'Excuse me, but you are the one suffering from denial here. You're denying your gross incompetence. But then I suppose they all look alike to you.' She pulled open another drawer. 'If he has been mislabelled I'll find him.'

'No you won't,' said Sandy who was standing over an opened drawer. 'This is the last one. He's not here.'

'Now, ladies, there's no point in upsetting yourselves further,' he said, silently praying that these two nutcases would go home and act like the recently bereaved are supposed to act.

'There is no further,' said Sandy. 'This is the max I can get upset. I don't even know where we go from here.'

'I should think that's obvious,' said Lauren. 'We go to the police.'

The two girls strode purposefully out of the room, leaving the coroner the unpleasant task of covering and putting away all the bodies.

As Lauren and Sandy left, neither of them noticed the tall dark man in the trenchcoat who had been lurking by the open doorway.

He had heard every word.

Chapter Eight

Sergeant O'Ryan sighed deeply to himself and not for the first time that day wished he were back out on the streets. He'd welcome tangling with some muggers, drug pushers or even the odd mass murderer: he could handle that. But sitting behind a desk dealing with all the hung-up weirdos New York could throw at him... that he couldn't cope with.

It was better in the good old days when his father had been a cop. Then the law was the law and people respected you, treated you with some awe. You gave as good as you got: it was tough but it was a man's world, a world of action and adventure.

And now here he was acting as some damn nursemaid to a couple of hyperactive and probably frustrated females who were spinning some wild story about missing bodies and mistaken identities.

Lauren interrupted his reverie. 'You see, the man in the morgue couldn't possibly be Michael,' she insisted. O'Ryan nodded politely. Wouldn't she ever shut up? Christ, he got off in half an hour. Couldn't they at least have waited till then?

'Michael has a strawberry-shaped birthmark...'

Sandy snorted with contempt. 'Its *not* a strawberry! It doesn't look anything like a strawberry!'

Lauren looked viciously at her. 'You're so knowledgeable,' she said through clenched teeth. 'What would you call it?'

'It's a liver spot,' she replied.

Lauren laughed superiorly. 'That was not a liver spot. Mottled, ancient, eighty-year-old people have liver spots . . .'

'It was this brown blob on his hip!'

'Stomach,' corrected Lauren. 'And it was not brown, it was dark pink.'

Over to you, Miss Brozinsky, thought O'Ryan.

Sandy shrugged. 'Brown, pink, what does it matter? We did it with the lights out . . .'

'Why, you little –' Lauren suddenly snapped and raised her fist, ready to land Sandy a most unladylike smack in the teeth.

At last faced with a situation he could understand and deal with, O'Ryan leapt from behind his desk. Shouting into the next office for assistance, he separated the two women. At the appearance of two burly female cops, Lauren and Sandy gave up and allowed themselves to be unceremoniously frogmarched out of the building.

'Oh, well done,' sneered Lauren when they were back out on the street. 'The very model of tact and decorum!'

'Who cares?' said Sandy as she gave the finger to the two female cops who stood watching them from the top of the steps leading into the police building. 'He wasn't going to help us anyway.'

'Why should he? You sounded insane!' Lauren sobbed involuntarily. 'God, it *is* insane! If he is alive, where is he?'

'He's probably back at my place wondering where the hell I am!' replied Sandy, not maliciously but simply stating what she believed.

'That I don't believe for one moment.'

Sandy rose to the bait. 'Boy, are you ever gonna shit cement!' she gloated and raised her hand to the oncoming traffic. 'Taxi!'

'If Michael is anywhere I assume he is in my apartment,' said Lauren. 'Taxi!'

They both stepped out into the road, looking this way and that for a yellow cab. As they did so, neither of them noticed the old garbage truck parked opposite them.

While they continued their argument a small aerial on the roof of the truck slowly swivelled around and pointed in their direction.

'You believe that, don't you?' Sandy asked Lauren. 'You believe he's at your place?'

Lauren hesitated before saying: 'I believe that he loved me, that he barely knew you, and that you're fantasising a relationship out of what was probably an isolated drunken encounter.'

Sandy was affronted. 'Isolated? *Isolated*? Listen, this girl does not have one night stands – no way! Every guy I've ever slept with has come back for more! Every one!'

Lauren and Sandy began to throw a torrent of abuse at each other. With every insult Sandy would thump Lauren on the shoulder, pushing her back against the wall. Passers-by scuttled past, trying not to notice; it was just another typical New York day.

'You want to hit me? Is that it?' taunted Lauren, obviously itching for a fight. 'All right. Try.'

Sandy took a step back and raised her fist. With a motion that would have put Sylvester Stallone to shame, she threw a savage right hook at Lauren – and hit thin air.

She looked around in disbelief. Lauren was standing some six feet away, gracefully completing a *grand jeté.*

She smiled patronisingly at her rival. 'Nine years of ballet,' she explained smugly.

Sandy, whose only experience of ballet had been a young dancer by the name of Ron, shook her head in defeat. 'You're too weird to hit...' she murmured. 'Taxi!'

'Look,' said Lauren reasonably. 'You insist he's in your apartment. I think he's in mine. So we'll go to both. If Michael's in your apartment – which I very much doubt – I will tell him goodbye. If, on the other hand, he is in my apartment, you will go off and find yourself a biker – and compare tatoos!'

Sandy considered. It was tough enough getting a cab in New York at the best of times. And what she wouldn't give to teach Miss Stuck-Up a lesson she'd never forget...

As a cab approached both girls dived into it. A few seconds after it moved away, the garbage truck revved up and drove off down the street.

Lauren and Sandy didn't know it but they were being followed.

Chapter Nine

'You see? He *is* here,' Lauren said triumphantly as she pushed open the unlocked door of her apartment. 'Now, I don't want a scene... you will try and be adult about this, won't you?'

Sandy motioned her to be quiet as they entered the hallway. There was a very good reason why Lauren's door was unlocked. Her apartment had been broken into.

The apartment was wrecked. Drawers had been opened, tables overturned, the bottoms of Lauren's chairs ripped. Books had been thrown recklessly around the apartment; even Lauren's precious Shakespearean posters had been torn down from the walls. Still searching through the debris were two sinister figures in trenchcoats. One of them was the man who had been spying on Lauren and Sandy at the morgue earlier.

Sandy pulled Lauren back into an alcove, out of view of the thieves. Lauren pressed herself against the wall, her pulse racing. 'Oh my God...' she whispered.

'Relax,' said Sandy, sounding slightly more nonchalant than she felt. 'It's just thieves.'

'*Russian* thieves?'

Sandy listened. Lauren was right: they were speaking Russian. One of them picked up an empty pouch of Michael's Colton's tobacco and sniffed it. He muttered something in Russian to his colleague.

Lauren turned in wide-eyed amazement to her companion. 'They're looking for Michael!'

'Lemme see!' Sandy leant forward for a better look and, as she did so, accidentally pushed Lauren out of the alcove and straight into a floor lamp which fell clattering to the ground.

The two men spun around at the noise. For a moment Lauren and Sandy stood there motionless, like two helpless mice face to face with a cat. Then, starting out of their shock, they turned and fled, slamming the door shut behind them.

They raced down the corridor of the apartment block as the men threw open the door and took chase. Out of the corner of her eyes Lauren saw them take two revolvers from their coat pockets. Oh dear God, she thought, this is it, this is the end.

The two shots rang out like thunderbolts. Both girls stopped instinctively in their tracks, each expecting to drop down dead.

Finding that they were still standing they turned around to see the two Russians fall down to the floor, tiny streams of blood trickling from the corners of their mouths. Behind them stood two other men – an older, sour-faced, sinister-looking character and a shorter, younger man with a weaselish expression. Each of them held smoking revolvers. It was they who had fired the shots and killed the two Russians.

'Oh my God!' squeaked Lauren as she looked down at the dead Russians.

Sandy was more practical. 'Now, who are *these*

assholes?' she asked, pointing to the two hitmen.

'How should I know?' asked Lauren. 'Run!'

As the two girls ran off the older man hesitated a second. 'Stop!' he cried out.

Not surprisingly Lauren and Sandy ignored his advice. The two men exchanged angry looks and then darted after the girls.

Lauren's heart pumped as never before as she tried to put as much distance between herself and her two pursuers. Her legs ached till she felt she couldn't go any further. Behind her Sandy flagged a little but was driven on by sheer fear and panic.

But as they ran along the corridor and down the stairs the men quickly began to catch up with them. Just as Lauren and Sandy thought they could go on no longer a door to one of the apartments opened and a little old lady dressed in chiffon and pearls came out carrying a bag of garbage to the rubbish chute.

Lauren and Sandy pushed her to one side, knocking the garbage out of her hands and raced gratefully into the apartment.

The apartment was a veritable aviary. It was packed with birds of all description, some in cages and some on perches. The floor was covered with spattered newspapers. As they dashed past them, they set up a deafening cacophony of outraged bird cries.

Their pursuers were not far behind. The bird lady had just picked up her garbage from the floor when they tore past her into the apartment. Deciding that she would never get used to living in New York City, she shook her head and pottered off with her garbage to the chute.

The two men stood in the middle of the room. Lauren and Sandy were nowhere to be seen. Fighting off the disgruntled cockatoos who were pecking away savagely at them, they ran to the open window and looked out.

Lauren and Sandy were scrambling down the outside fire escape. The older man rapped an order and he and his colleague took up the chase again.

Lauren and Sandy reached the end of the fire escape which was still a full storey off the ground. They tugged at the lever which would release the ladder and enable them to climb down to safety.

'Stuck!' Sandy cursed under her breath.

'What do we do now?' cried Lauren, pointing up at their pursuers who were almost upon them. 'They're going to kill us!'

'In here,' said Sandy, wrenching open a window by the fire escape. 'Quick!'

The window led into the apartment block's laundry room. Lauren and Sandy found themselves surrounded by a dozen whirring washing machines and dryers. They looked around desperately. No place to hide.

Moments later their pursuers clambered in through the window. There was no sign of Lauren and Sandy.

'Look, what do we want those bimbos for, Mr Atkins?' asked the Weasel. 'What do they know?'

'They know he survived. They may know where he is. Come on, they're not here, let's try upstairs.'

They stalked out of the room, closing the door behind them. A few minutes' silence passed and then the top of one of the dryers opened up to display a mass of red hair topped with a frilly lace brassiere. Sandy looked around cautiously and then tapped on the lid of the adjacent dryer.

Lauren opened the dryer in which she had been hiding. She looked even worse than Sandy. Her hair was dishevelled and her face was a distinct shade of green;

various items of clothing stuck to her body.

Sandy grinned at her. 'Well, so much for your apartment! Wanna try mine?'

Chapter Ten

With their hair and clothes awry, a glazed look of fear and astonishment still in their eyes, and with a stray sock clinging to Lauren's back, Lauren and Sandy looked perfectly at home with the other weirdos travelling the New York subway.

As the train rattled on its way to Sandy's apartment on the Lower East Side, Lauren buried her face in her hands.

'I don't believe this,' she said to Sandy. 'Did you hear what they said? "They know he survived!" I think they're the ones who tried to kill him in the explosion! Why would anyone want to kill a schoolteacher?'

'It's the four F's! Fluoride, Fast Food and Fornication!' offered a helpful drunk at the other end of the carriage.

'That's about as good an answer as I can give,' Sandy admitted.

'Would you be serious for a moment!' snapped Lauren. 'Michael is in some kind of serious trouble!'

'That's why you don't see half dollars anymore,' continued the drunk.

Sandy ignored him. 'Chill out,' she advised Lauren.

'It'll soon be over, OK?'

'How? It might just have escaped your notice, but we do have two sets of homicidal maniacs after us,' Lauren reminded her.

'One,' corrected Sandy. 'One set killed the other set, remember?'

'Oh, well, that makes me feel much better,' Lauren said with all the sarcasm she could muster.

'It'll be over because Michael will be at my apartment,' Sandy said vehemently, 'and he will tell you what's going on and you will make good your deal and get lost forever and this will be over!'

'Wouldn't've happened if Nixon was still alive!' the drunk said.

Lauren turned disdainfully to the drunk and then back to Sandy. 'I hate public transport,' she said with a scornful sniff.

Chapter Eleven

Sandy's apartment was in a worse state than Lauren's. Clothes were strewn all over the floor, drawers had been upturned and searched through; piles of clothes littered the floor and the bathroom door hung off its hinges.

Lauren was about to back out when Sandy stopped her. 'Relax,' she reassured her. 'This is normal –'

Picking her way through the rubble she entered the apartment, calling out Michael's name.

No reply.

'He's not here,' said Sandy, clearly surprised. Before Lauren had a chance to say anything she warned her: 'Don't gloat – don't. Just get out.'

'If you don't mind I'd like to use your phone,' Lauren said. 'I need a place to hide first. Do you have a phone? Or have they finally cut you off?'

'No way,' said Sandy and began to dig through a pile of discarded clothes. 'Howie's my buddy.' With not a little trouble she eventually found the phone which had been buried under a pile of underwear. She was about to give it to Lauren when she suddenly snatched it back.

'Wait a minute – I need a place to hide too. Those guys are probably on their way here.' Hurriedly she dialled a number. 'Hi, Alan,' she said when she was connected. 'Can I sleep at your place tonight? Great! What d'you mean, where? On the couch... Now come on, Alan, that's all over for us... *because*! Hello? Hello?'

She hung up the phone, cursing under her breath. Lauren grabbed the phone from her and dialled a number.

'Hello, Mom,' she began. 'I need a favour ... no! Not –' It was too late. With a sigh Lauren replaced the reveiver. 'I have a problem with my parents,' she explained.

'So call one of your girlfriends,' suggested Sandy.

'I don't have girlfriends.'

'Figures.'

Exasperated Lauren turned to go. Sandy stopped her. 'Where are you off to?' she demanded.

There was a look of grim determination on Lauren's face. 'Michael's in trouble. I am going to find him.'

'Oh yeah? Where?'

'He could be hiding, he could he hurt – oh, I don't know!' she cried, realising she had no idea where he might be. 'All I know is that he needs my help. Now, please excuse me.'

She tried to brush past Sandy but Sandy held her ground. 'Where're you gonna look? In his apartment? You think he's gonna be hanging out at his apartment when someone wants to kill him?'

'I'm not going to his apartment,' Lauren said, sounding just like a little kid trying to keep a secret.

'Then where?'

'Isn't that *my* business?' Lauren asked. Sandy clearly thought it wasn't.

'Look – if you have any idea you might as well tell me and we'll go and find him right now and help him out of this!' She thought a moment and then added: 'And then we'll make him choose.'

'Choose? Between us?' Lauren laughed cruelly. 'I doubt he'll even remember your name.'

Sandy smirked defiantly. 'You're so goddamn sure it's gonna be you, what do you care?'

'I'm confident, yes,' Lauren said evenly.

For a few seconds Sandy hesitated, looking at Lauren's slim ladylike figure. Then she snapped herself out of any doubt she might have had. 'Right! Let's go! she said, leading her way out of the apartment.

She paused at the door and adjusted her hair in the mirror. Then she picked up a huge dazzling rhinestone from a nearby table and attached it to her left earlobe.

'What *is* that?' Lauren enquired sarcastically, marvelling at Sandy's sheer lack of good taste.

Sandy grinned. 'Got it off the Christmas tree at Saks,' she answered. 'Don't worry – nobody saw.'

'Well, if you want to look like a Gabor sister I suppose that's your business.'

'I should be so lucky. Now, where are we going?'

Chapter Twelve

Lauren and Sandy felt distinctly out of place in the tobacco store as they stood waiting to be served. The air was heavy with the heady aroma of hundreds of different kinds of tobacco. The entire shop reeked of masculinity.

'You are such a douche bag,' Sandy told Lauren. 'The man's afraid for his life; he's not gonna stop and buy tobacco.'

'Obviously you didn't spend the sort of time with him that I did,' Lauren retorted haughtily. 'He wouldn't be able to last a day without his Colton's and this is the only place in town that stocks it.'

Sandy nodded, impressed by Lauren's reasoning, as she continued: 'Now, this time would you please let me handle this? Your simplest exchanges with people become pornographic.'

His sale completed, the sales assistant turned his attention to the two women. He eyed them up lasciviously as Lauren gave him her most dazzling smile. 'How can I help you, miss?' he asked with a leer. He sounded and looked just like Benny Hill.

'Er, we're looking for a friend of ours – he comes in here quite often to buy his tobacco.' Lauren proceeded to give the clerk a detailed description of Michael.

'Yeah, I know the guy,' the clerk nodded.

'Was he in here today?' asked Lauren just a little too eagerly. 'Have you seen him?'

The clerk sized her up, lingering a moment too long on her shapely legs. 'Maybe ... maybe not ...'

'When do you think you'll arrive at a decision?' she asked calmly, trying to conceal her growing impatience and irritation.

'Over a drink?' he suggested hopefully.

Lauren tried to hide her repulsion at the thought of even being seen in the same bar as this creep. 'Wouldn't you feel better as a person' – she paused at the word, wondering if it could be applied to the clerk – 'just unselfishly helping someone find out something she'd really like to know?'

'Nope. How about dinner?'

Sandy strolled up to the counter, thrusting her breasts forward and wiggling her hips in a suggestive manner. 'How about a BJ?' she asked.

The clerk froze. 'A what?' he croaked, not believing his ears.

'You know what a BJ stands for,' Sandy continued. 'Right here. Right now. Both of us – taking turns.'

Lauren stood by speechless with horror at what Sandy was suggesting. The clerk, on the other hand, rubbed his sweaty palms together, eyeing up each girl in turn. His tongue was practically hanging out of his mouth. Suddenly he was eager to help them in any way he could.

'He was in here this afternoon,' he said.

'You're sure it was this afternoon?' asked Sandy.

The clerk nodded. Sandy and Lauren exchanged excited looks: Michael was alive!

'Yeah, one o'clock. He bought ten pouches of

Colton's.'

'What else?'

'Nothing. He was kinda in a hurry. He used the phone and then ran out of here.'

'He used the phone at one,' repeated Sandy thoughtfully. 'OK, is that it?'

'Sure is, baby.' The clerk smiled and walked over to the store window to pull down the shade. Lauren gazed on in horror at the expectant bulge in his trousers. Sandy, however, smiled back invitingly at the randy clerk. My God, thought Lauren, she's actually going to go through with it and she expects me to –

'Here, or in the back?' asked the clerk.

'I think I can take care of it from here,' Sandy whispered seductively.

The clerk was positively quivering with excitement. He closed his eyes in anticipation and began to unbutton his trousers. With teasing theatricality Sandy blew him a kiss – and then grabbed a stunned Lauren and raced out into the street.

'That was the most disgusting, unscrupulous thing I ever saw in my entire life,' Lauren protested as she and Sandy sprinted round the street corner, the tobacco clerk's curses still ringing in their ears.

'What's your problem now?' demanded Sandy as they stopped by an empty phone booth.

'Promising sexual favours, that's what's wrong!' Lauren said indignantly. 'That sends us back to the Dark Ages. It is something that you don't do!'

Sandy shrugged. 'You do if you're lying . . . Besides, it worked.' She went into the phone booth, inserted her money and then dialled a number.

'Excuse me, but I have missed something,' continued

Lauren. 'How exactly did it work? We're at a dead end!'

Sandy urged her to shut up as she made her connection. She asked for Howie Rinker and then smiled as he came on the line. 'Sandy here, Howie! Yeah, great, what about you? How's your fish? What did the vet say?'

Lauren was at a loss to see what importance the phone clerk's diseased fish had and said so. Sandy ignored her and continued her conversation. 'Listen, Howie cutie – being as you're my main man at the phone company I need a teensy-weensy favour. Can you tell me what number was called out of Louis's Pipe and Tobacco Company at one o'clock this afternoon?' As she waited she put her hand over the receiver and said to Lauren: 'Howie's sweet but he's probably one of those guys with polyester pants and hips – yuk! Oh, hi, I'm here . . . Good boy! That's a cab company, right?'

She grabbed a pencil and scrap of paper out of her bag and began to scribble. 'Got it, Howie! You're a catch! Our kids're gonna be gorgeous!' She smacked a few long wet kisses down the phone and hung up.

There was a wide grin on her face as she turned back to Lauren. Lauren surprised herself by returning the grin.

'Don't smirk,' she said, taking the piece of paper from Sandy. 'Let me see too.'

As she looked at the address on the paper Sandy was urgently hailing down a cab. At last they were on Michael's trail.

Chapter Thirteen

The address Howie had given Sandy was a seedy cab company on the West Side of Central Park. As they got out of the cab Lauren looked around uneasily: if her mother could see her now she'd probably have a major cardiac arrest.

In the centre of the oil-spattered parking bay a group of burly Negros and Puerto Ricans sat around a table, playing a serious crap game. Ghetto blasters pounded out an unending stream of funk as the cabbies swigged back cans of Budweiser and smoked peculiar smelling rolled-up cigarettes. It was a place out of Lauren's wildest nightmares, but to Sandy it was just little ol' uptown New York.

While Lauren wondered how she'd ever got in this mess in the first place, Sandy marched up to the despatcher's cage. Inside, a fat balding little man was flipping through an old issue of *Penthouse*.

'Hi,' said Sandy, playing the dizzy female. The despatcher looked up at her through narrow stoat-like eyes.

'God, I am such a ditz,' Sandy continued. 'I left my tennis racquet in one of your cabs today. Pick-up would have been Broadway and 77th around one o'clock.

'There a reward?' he asked.

'Yes,' she said quickly before Lauren had a chance to put her foot in it.

As the despatcher leafed through his log book, a fight broke out at the nearby table. A tall hulking black guy who could have eaten Arnold Schwarzenegger for breakfast and sill have room left over for Chuck Norris, was setting on an equally muscular Puerto Rican.

The despatcher looked unperturbed and shouted out. The hulk halted in mid-punch and turned around. 'That's your man,' he said to the two wary women.

'Your turn now,' Sandy whispered to Lauren.

Lauren gulped. 'I don't know how to talk to him!' she protested in a horrid tone. 'I went to a private school!'

'Ah, he'll love you!' Sandy pushed her forward.

Lauren smiled at the hulk and tried to remember how they went about this sort of thing in *Hill Street Blues*. 'Hi, I wanted to ask you about a fare you had this morning,' she began. 'A very good-looking Cauca – er, just person will do . . . I mean, why differentiate?' Behind her Sandy raised her eyes in disbelief. How the hell had Lauren survived New York for one day, let alone twenty years?

'You picked him up outside a little smoke shop . . .' Lauren went on. 'Does that ring any bell whatsoever?'

'Tall guy?' asked the hulk.

'Yes!'

'Blue coat?'

'Yes, yes! That's him!'

'Don't remember a thing,' he said definitely.

Lauren was confused. 'But you just said . . .'

'I didn't say nothin'.'

'Now, don't give me a big song and dance –' Lauren stopped, realising what she was saying. The hulk began to advance threateningly on her.

'What the hell is the matter with you?' Sandy hissed as she pulled Lauren back. 'Why should he help you if there's nothing in it for him?'

'All right then, you tell me what I'm supposed to do!'

'You're an actress – bullshit him!

'I am *not* using my training to tell *lies* to people,' Lauren snorted self-importantly.

Sandy gave up. 'What do you use it for then? Jesus, it's so simple – watch!'

Sandy strode confidently up to the hulk. 'Wanna make a quick two hundred?' she asked. The hulk raised an eyebrow: he was interested. Sandy continued: 'Two hundred bucks in cash. Just take us where you took the guy.'

The hulk stood there for a moment, pretending to consider Sandy's offer. Then he sauntered over to his cab and with just a hint of sarcasm opened the back door for the women and invited them to climb aboard.

'Are you insane?' Lauren whispered to Sandy. 'Where are we going to get two hundred bucks?'

'Get in the cab,' Sandy ordered through clenched teeth.

Lauren shook her head defiantly. 'This is unacceptable, I do not accept this,' she ranted. 'I am *not* getting in that cab!'

A quarter of an hour later and despite Lauren's vociferous protests the two girls were sitting in the back of the cab and looking out onto a scene of utter devastation. The hulk had driven them to a hell on Earth. Everywhere there were burnt-out tenement buildings, wrecked cars, broken windows. Tribes of what appeared to be neolithic savages fought and ran though the garbage and the shit. Here and there a few derelicts wandered purposelessly about, skilfully picking their way around the other tramps who were too drunk to notice. To Lauren, it seemed like the aftermath of a nuclear blast.

It was, in fact, Harlem.

'Where are we?' Lauren asked nervously. 'We've been going for miles and I haven't seen a single white person on the street.'

'There's one,' piped up Sandy. 'Whoops! They just got him!

'That isn't funny...'

The cab stopped outside a particularly evil-looking tenement. The girls' faces fell.

'You're sure this is it?' Sandy asked the driver.

The hulk didn't answer but turned around and held out his hand. He wanted his two hundred dollars now.

'Keep your pants on,' Sandy said irritably. 'I'm not through with you. Wait here.'

She reached for the door handle but the hulk grabbed her collar, yanking her back. He stared menacingly into her eyes, but Sandy kept her cool.

'Look, asshole, you and I know that I'm never gonna get another cab to come out here to Viet Nam, so get real!'

No response. Sandy sighed and gave in: 'All right, all right. Three hundred bucks to stay right here until we come back.' The hulk released his grip and Sandy and Lauren gratefully got out of the cab. 'You're a pain in the ass, you know that?' Sandy called back to him as they approached the tenement.

'You are beyond belief!' exploded Lauren when they were safely out of the hulk's earshot. 'I would like to point out that we do not have thirty dollars between us, let alone three hundred! You are really determined to have us both killed!'

'Oh, relax,' said Sandy. 'He's not gonna kill us.'

'Really? Whyever not?'

''Cause we're gonna be raped and murdered in this building!' Sandy said simply and pushed open the front door.

Chapter Fourteen

The lobby of the tenement was a sad indictment of New York society. The place stank like a sewer. The walls were sprayed with obscene graffitti, the signs of rival gangs. There were blood stains on the floor and rats scampered among the garbage and shit. As Lauren and Sandy made their way through the lobby they were careful to avoid the gaping holes in the floor.

Suddenly they froze as they heard behind them an unmistakable *click!* Very, very slowly they turned around.

Facing them was a little Puerto Rican kid, dressed in a baseball cap, t-shirt, jeans and sneakers, just like any other normal kid. Unlike most other normal kids, he was also pointing a loaded gun directly at Lauren and Sandy.

'My God, he's a child!' gasped Lauren.

Sandy looked on the bright side. 'Well, at least rape's out . . .'

Lauren shot her an angry glance. 'Let me handle this, I've always had a way with children,' she said and made to bend down to the kid's level. 'Now, should you really be playing with your daddy's –'

'Don't move or I foockin' kill you!'

Lauren jumped back startled, but soon discovered her sense of indignation. 'Now, I've just had about enough of this, young man,' she hectored like some aging schoolmarm. 'You put that thing down now before you put someone's eye out!'

'Oh, great,' despaired Sandy, 'like he's really gonna respond to Ward Cleaver!'

'Your bags – throw them over here,' commanded the young thug.

Reluctantly Lauren and Sandy tossed him their purses. 'Have you ever robbed actresses before?' Lauren asked seriously. 'This isn't going to be exactly the most satisfying haul of your career.'

The kid searched through their bags with growing annoyance. 'Where is your money?' he demanded. 'Your credit cards?'

Jesus, thought Sandy, the kid had a lot to learn. 'Revoked! Where do you think!'

The kid cursed in Spanish and stamped his foot with all the natural petulance of a nine-year-old who can't get what he wants. As he hopped up and down in rage, he waved the gun menacingly in Sandy's face.

Suddenly a sinister *thunk!* caused Lauren to scream. The gun had gone off right in Sandy's stomach.

'Oh my God!' she cried. 'You've *killed* her!'

Sandy stood still, her face drained. There was something not quite right about this. It had a lot to do with the fact that she hadn't fallen to the ground in a bloody mess.

Cautiously she felt her stomach and then her chest. 'I'm not dead!' she yelped, and at the same instant lunged at the kid. With Lauren's help she pinned him to the wall and relieved him of his gun.

'I'll be damned,' she said with something approaching

admiration. 'It's a fake!' She passed Lauren the gun; in every respect, even its weight and noise, it was a perfect replica of a Colt 45. No one would have been able to tell the difference between it and the real thing. 'Look at the detail,' she said appreciatively. 'It's incredible workmanship.'

She turned to the kid who was standing sulkily in a corner of the room. 'Where did you get this?'

'Santa.'

Lauren bent down, once again playing the role of the sympathetic grown-up. 'We're looking for a friend of ours,' she said. 'If you can help us we'll let you have your toy back.'

She described Michael in detail. The kid nodded and led them up the stairs to the second floor. He indicated a locked door.

'He came here,' he said.

'Yeah, but did he come out?' Sandy wondered aloud. She pressed an ear to the door and heard the sound of raucous music coming from inside. With a look which said 'it's now or never' she knocked on the door.

'Maybe they can't hear us,' suggested Lauren when there was no reply.

'Well, we can't stand here all day,' Sandy said resignedly and bent down to the lock. Taking a hair pin from out of her hair she stuck it in the lock and began to twist it. The pin broke immediately.

By her side the Puerto Rican kid burst out laughing. Sandy shot him a look of pure poison. 'OK, so what's *your* idea?'

The kid waved the two amateurs aside and from out of his pocket took a curious many-pronged fork. In one deft movement he had inserted it into the lock and turned it. The door clicked open.

He looked up at Lauren and Sandy. There was a superior smirk on his face. Beaming with admiration, Sandy ruffled his hair. 'You little thug,' she said affectionately.

'Can I have my gun back now?' he asked.

'Dream on, kid.' With a smart pat on his rear Sandy sent him on his way.

Slowly Lauren and Sandy opened the door and crept into the room beyond...

Chapter Fifteen

It could almost have been a scene out of *Miami Vice*.

Inside the room two men were hunched over a rickety kitchen table. On the table was a scale upon which was placed a pound of white powder. Small plastic bags of the same powder were also scattered about the table.

To their right on a threadbare couch was a pile of automatic weapons. It was clear that the men were involved in a major high-powered and also highly illegal drugs transaction – and they most definitely did not want to be disturbed.

As soon as they heard the door creak open they bounded to their feet and turned to face the women. Lauren and Sandy gulped: something told them that this was the wrong time to make an entrance. These men were killers: they didn't stand a chance.

Suddenly – to both her and Sandy's complete astonishment – Lauren sprang forward. With her feet placed firmly apart she pointed the little kid's toy gun straight at the two hoods.

'Police!' she cried in a thick Bronx accent. 'Yuh under arrest!'

The men froze. They looked over to the weapons on

the couch.

'Don't think about it!' bawled Lauren. 'Don't even fuckin' think about it or I'll blow yuh nuts off!'

Sandy stared in dumbstruck amazement. Was this the Miss Prim And Proper she knew and loathed and who blanched at the thought of portraying even a whore on stage, let alone a maniacal cop?

'OK? Do we understand each other?' Lauren continued. 'Turn around! Face the wall! Do it now!'

Sandy still couldn't believe what was happening. Here was Lauren suddenly doing a Cagney and Lacey and these two hardened crooks were actually obeying her. Maybe Lauren wasn't such a bad actress after all.

'Frisk them,' Lauren ordered Sandy. Cautiously, Sandy approached the quaking villains and ran her hands distastefully over their bodies. A collection of knives clattered noisily to the floor. She picked them up and together with the weapons on the couch flung them down the airshaft.

'OK. Now read them their rights,' ordered Policewoman Lauren Ames.

Sandy looked at her as though she'd gone crazy. What was she playing at now? They'd got the weapons; now, let's get the hell out of here, Tonto. But faced with no other choice Sandy complied: 'Yeah... you have the right to... uh... remain silent. Anything you say can and will be used against you... uh...' Shit, what was it Kojak used to say?

'Attorney!' Lauren whispered.

'Yeah! You have the right to an attorney...'

'OK, OK, I've heard it all before,' the first dealer said as Sandy dried up.

'What do you want?' asked his companion. 'Whatever you want we got it!'

'That's right!' agreed the first dealer. 'We can cut you a sweet deal!'

'Yeah, yeah, we've heard it all before,' said Lauren, echoing the dealer.

'Hey, maybe they can help us find Sanders,' Sandy suggested, suddenly tuning into Lauren's plan.

'They don't know Sanders.'

'Michael Sanders?' said the first dealer, eager to do whatever he could to save his skin. 'Yeah, he was here a coupla hours ago. Ray here fixed him up with a fake passport.'

'Fuck you, Gilroy,' said Ray.

'Oh, so we're in the phony ID business now?' said Lauren, getting carried away with a role once more. 'That's nice . . .'

'I wanna see a lawyer,' Ray demanded.

Lauren put the gun against his head. 'You're not gonna have much of a conversation. They'll hafta squeegee your face off the wall first!'

'She gets kinda kranky,' Sandy offered helpfully. 'Better tell us the name.'

'J-John Strauss,' Ray stammered.

'Where'd he go?'

'I don't know. He was leaving town, that's all!' Wouldn't these two pigs ever leave him alone? He pointed to a small briefcase by the table. 'Look, I'm being real nice. Why don't you be nice too? Open that box – go on!'

Sandy went over and gingerly opened it. It was packed full of one hundred dollar bills.

'Why don't you just keep it and forget we ever met?'

Lauren and Sandy looked at each other thoughtfully. After all, they did have a homicidal cab driver waiting outside for his fare . . .

*

Minutes later, Lauren and Sandy walked safely out of the tenement and back to the waiting cab. Sandy was hugging the case of money like an overjoyed little girl.

'Well, I'm gonna have to give you that one, kid. You were – Lauren? Lauren?'

She turned around. Lauren had collapsed on the floor in a dead faint.

Chapter Sixteen

'A deal's a deal,' said Sandy as their cab drew up to the airport terminal building. With an exaggerated flourish she pulled three one hundred dollar bills out of the case and handed them to the cab driver. She pushed open the door and dragged a still dazed Lauren out after her.

As they passed into the terminal building they failed to see a group of five or six men, all of whom were carrying walkie-talkies. Their leader gave them each their instructions and then they quickly disappeared into different directions.

They were not airport security personnel.

If Lauren and Sandy had noticed them they would have recognised their leader instantly: it was Atkins, the same man who had killed the Russians and chased Lauren and Sandy through the corridors of Lauren's apartment building.

'They won't give out passenger lists,' Lauren said despondently as she left the departures counter. 'You've got to be either police or FBI.'

Lauren might be a good actress, thought Sandy, but she sure as hell had a lot to learn about human nature.

She pointed to the case of money she held in her hand and gave it to Lauren. 'You are such a dip!' she said. 'This is all the ID we need.'

'You think so?' asked Lauren, indicating the woman on the next counter. 'Does that look like the sort of woman who can be bribed?'

The official at the booking desk looked like Arnold Schwarzenegger in skirts. It would have taken the combined might of the Gestapo, the KGB and the Dirty Dozen to get a smile, let alone a little information out of her.

Sandy knew when she was defeated. 'OK, so what's your idea?'

Lauren thought for a moment. Taking a deep breath, she pushed Sandy aside and walked over to the desk.

'Excuse me . . .' she began timidly.

'Yes?'

'Yes, hello,' Lauren fumbled on: her face distraught with anxiety, 'I vas hoped perhaps you vould to help me . . . My vather . . . ach, how you say? . . .'

'You say it quickly,' said the woman, drumming her fingers impatiently on the top of the desk. 'I'm off in three minutes.'

'My vather . . . no . . . I vill tell from beginning. I am Anna and this is my sister Elona.' She pointed at Sandy.

Sandy opened her mouth to speak, but Lauren silenced her. 'She does not know English,' she said hurriedly. 'Our vather ve have not seen since ve vas babies in Prague . . . He send us to to Hungary during Dubritchka – ve vas in suitcase in train – ve escape . . . you see . . .'

'No, I'm afraid I don't,' the woman said steely.

'Now ve get letter– he escape also – he is here – but nobody tell us vat plane – could be any plane . . . Please tell . . .'

'Sorry. Police and FBI only.' The response was automatic and final.

Lauren's face fell into a well-rehearsed mask of Chekhovian devastation and disappointment. With tears in her eyes she turned to 'Elona' and explained the situation in pseudo-Czechoslovakian gibberish. Sandy responded in the same gibberish, affecting a face of acute dismay. Then with a flourish which even Ethel Barrymore would have been proud of Lauren fell sobbing into Sandy's arms.

After what she felt was a respectable period of heartfelt hysteria she looked hopefully back at the woman on the desk. She sat there unmoved; but wasn't there a trace of a smile upon her lips?

'Nice try,' the Amazon at the desk said.

Lauren was deeply offended. '*Nice try*!' she exploded, forgetting her Czechoslovakian accent. 'That was damn good! You should have bought that!'

'Oh, I was thoroughly entertained. I wanted to be an actress myself once. Too tall.' She gave Lauren and Sandy an unexpected warm smile. 'Now, what was the name?'

Lauren beamed. 'Strauss. John Strauss.'

The woman turned to the computer terminal at her side and pushed a few keys. She read aloud the information displayed on the screen. 'Here we go: John Strauss: Flight 501 to Albuquerque. Looks like you just missed him.'

Lauren and Sandy exchanged a look of despair. They'd come too far not to miss Michael now.

'Keep your pants on though,' the woman said, punching in more numbers. 'If you hurry you can catch United 1212 and change in Atlanta. You've got a shorter stopover so you can beat him. You want a ticket?'

The girls nodded excitedly and opened the case. The woman looked suspiciously at the money but said nothing as she accepted their fare and made out two tickets.

Delighted with the way things suddenly seemed to be going in their favour Lauren and Sandy turned – to see Atkins and the Weasel staring at them from the other end of the hall.

For a second neither party moved. Then in a sudden burst, Lauren made a run for an exit door which led into a long corridor. Atkins and the Weasel ran after her, forgetting in the heat of the moment Sandy, who grabbed the tickets and ran off in the opposite direction.

Lauren ran as fast as her legs would carry her, faster than she had ever done before in her life. By her side the money case impeded her progress while all the while her pursuers came closer and closer.

As she sped up and down the escalators and along moving sidewalks, she weaved in and out of startled passengers, making maximum use of them to hinder her pursuers.

But still they came closer and closer. Lauren's heart pumped frantically as she tried to force her failing legs to run once more.

With Atkins and the Weasel only about twenty yards behind her, she finally reached the departure area. Pushing her way through the line of passengers who were dutifully waiting at the security check point she leapt through the metal scanners and towards the departure gate.

Seconds later her pursuers passed through the same scanners. Alarm bells began to clang through the terminal. Airport security, suspecting at the very least a terrorist attack, joined in the chase.

At the departure gate a very worried Sandy was trying to persuade the airline official to delay the flight just one more minute.

'I swear she'll be here any second now,' she said desperately. 'Her IV got caught in the luggage rack.'

The official shook his head and attempted to rope off the departure gate, but Sandy tried one more time.

'She can't miss this plane!' she pleaded. 'She's a sick woman! There's a kidney in Kansas City which isn't getting any fresher!'

Lauren was now within sight of the departure gate and her eyes could just make out the figure of Sandy arguing with the airline official.

She looked behind her. There was only ten yards between her and Atkins and the Weasel now. Within seconds they would be upon her. It looked like this was it . . . unless . . .

Still running, she undid the catch of the briefcase and flung its contents up into the air.

Hundreds and hundreds of dollar bills rained down like manna from heaven. Seemingly out of nowhere, people appeared, greedily grabbing the bills, leaping into the air, diving to the ground. In effect, they created an impenetrable wall between Lauren and her pursuers.

Summoning up new reserves of energy Lauren jumped over the rope and sprinted through the departure gate.

'About time too!' Sandy cried with relief and ran after her.

A totally bemused airline official called after her:

'*That's* your sick aunt?'

Sandy turned back to him. 'It's a miracle!' she cried gratefully.

Chapter Seventeen

Safe in the airborne plane to Albuquerque an exhausted Lauren lay back in her seat, apparently fast asleep. By her side, Sandy was very much awake. She had been staring hatefully at Lauren for the past ten minutes.

Even if Lauren had been asleep that hate would have woken her. Her eyes opened. 'OK – what is it?' she asked.

'That was all our money,' Sandy told her.

'Oh well, pardon me: I guess you'd rather have us rich and dead.'

'You could've left us with one little shitty dollar,' complained Sandy as she leant back in her seat. 'The only thing in the world I need right now is a drink.'

Lauren sighed. She knew just what Sandy meant. 'Yeah,' she said longingly, 'a drink would be marvellous.'

'Well, then, what'll it be, you pretty little fillies?' asked a strong Southern drawl.

Startled, Lauren and Sandy looked across the aisle at the ruddy-faced Texan who was easing himself into his seat. He was wearing a shiny three-piece suit which on the right person would have looked trendily kitsch; on him it just looked ridiculous. He waved over the stewardess who was approaching with the drinks tray.

'Get on down here, honey!' he hollered out. 'These girls're in sore need.' He winked at Lauren and Sandy and then nodded over to the passenger sitting next to him. 'My friend Dale here has gone his limit, an' I do so hate to imbibe alone.'

Lauren and Sandy returned his attentions with a frozen smile as he continued: 'You gotta pace yourself at a convention, that's for sure. Now, what's your pleasure?'

'Scotch,' Sandy replied automatically.

'Vodka tonic,' said Lauren and then checked herself. 'No, forget the tonic. On the rocks – a double . . .'

Sandy gave Lauren a curious look. Lauren shrugged. To hell with principles, she needed a drink.

The stewardess came over and poured them their drinks. The girls gulped them eagerly.

'I'm Al Gurney of Al's Albuquerque Ford,' the Texan offered. The girls mumbled their names. 'Sandra and Laura,' he repeated. 'Pretty names for pretty girls. Oh no, now I know you like to be called women, don't you? You'll have to forgive an old tomcat!'

Lauren and Sandy gave each other a look as if to say 'Who is this jerk?' But in the true spirit of dramatic improvisation they smiled sweetly at him and raised their drinks in a toast.

An hour later, Lauren and Sandy's plastic trays were cluttered with a collection of empty scotch and vodka miniatures. Al, on his third Bloody Mary, was getting decidedly friendly with the girls, as well as successfully boring the hell out of them.

Sandy was flicking through a brochure featuring the

latest Ford models, less out of interest and more to escape conversation with the lecherous old Texan.

'See, most dealers get to order the vehicle of their choice,' he droned on, 'and it's pot luck as far as the colour goes. Now *I* can put you in a Turbo Z any colour of the rainbow – maroon, you name it, you drive it away this afternoon.'

Lauren judged by the silence that it was her turn to speak. 'I don't know,' she murmured evasively, hoping that that was a suitable reply to whatever Al was rambling on about.

'Financin' botherin' you?' asked the helpful Texan. 'Hell, I don't care if you're a housewife or a secretary, there's no deal that can't be made.'

You would care if you knew I was an actress, thought Lauren.

'I don't know, Laura,' Sandy said wickedly, leaning over and showing Lauren a page on the Ford brochure. 'This Tempo looks pretty snappy.' Let her get out of that one, she thought.

'What colour do you want?' Al asked, seizing the opportunity. 'Maroon?'

I hate goddamn maroon, thought Lauren. 'I really don't know,' she said.

'All right,' Al conceeded. 'You gals like steak and lobster?'

'Love it!' cried Sandy, licking her lips.

Lauren was horrified at the implications of going out to dinner with this creature. 'No!' she cried.

'Laura,' persisted Al, 'I think there's an apricot margarita with your name on it.' He winked suggestively at her.

Sandy put a finger to Lauren's lips as she began to protest. 'Look, there may be more of those guys waiting for us,' she whispered in her ear. 'If there are, they're gonna be looking for two *single* women! This is our ticket off the plane!'

Lauren smiled weakly at Al's beaming red face. What had she said earlier about the promise of sexual favours sending women back to the Dark Ages?

She weighed up the alternatives in her mind. There was no contest: it was welcome back to the Dark Ages.

Turning to Sandy, she whispered: 'All right. *You* get the drunk one.'

Flight 127 from Atlanta made a perfect touch down at Albuquerque and slowed to a halt outside the terminal building. From their vantage point on one of the observation decks two sinister men in black glasses and clutching walkie talkies observed the disembarking passengers as they walked down the stairway and across the tarmac to the arrivals lounge.

Lauren was walking arm in arm with Al, chatting merrily away about wheelbase specifications and dual radials. She hoped her phoney look of affection would be at least enough to convince people that they were man and mistress, if not man and wife. Following them were Sandy and Dale, who was leaning heavily against her for support. In total contrast to Lauren, Sandy's face indicated that she was thoroughly pisssed off with Dale and his drunken fumbles.

As they approached the terminal building a sleek private Lear jet came gliding slowly to a halt about fifty yards in front of them. Lauren and Sandy exchanged worried glances: some feminine sixth sense told them they were not out of trouble yet. A murmur of silent agreement passed between them.

'Now where are you scooting off to?' cried Al. 'Hey!

Come back!'

But it was too late. Lauren and Sandy had already detached themselves from Al and Dale and were running as fast as they could across the landing field.

Lauren and Sandy's intuition had served them well. The Lear jet came to a final halt and the hatchway opened to reveal the men who had spied on the girls earlier. As they climbed out they looked around them, but they could see no sign of Lauren or Sandy.

Last to leave was Atkins himself who promptly ordered the men to follow the passengers off the Atlanta flight and into the terminal building.

As his men obeyed his orders, Atkins made to follow. But then, like Lauren and Sandy before him, some special sense made him hesitate. His eyes searched the landing field until they came to rest on a cart piled high with passengers' luggage. Baggage handlers were unloading suitcases one by one onto a moving belt which led off into the baggage reclaim area within the terminal building.

He was about to turn away when he saw the baggage handlers remove two particularly large suitcases and reveal, crouched behind them, Lauren and Sandy.

Their eyes locked and then with a yelp of panic the two girls leapt out of their hiding place and jumped onto the moving conveyor belt. Frantically they pushed suitcases out of their way and climbed over the heavier baggage, making their way towards the narrow portal which led into the terminal building.

Atkins gave immediate chase and sprinted over to the conveyor belt just as Lauren and Sandy disappeared from view. Jumping onto the moving belt, he clambered over the items of baggage following the two fleeing women.

In the baggage reclaim area a group of tired passengers were waiting impatiently for their baggage to arrive on the carousel. One particularly frustrated woman was firing a torrent of complaint at her long-suffering husband.

'You noticed the people from First Class got their bags straight away?' she whined in a grating monotone. 'My legs are still asleep – I felt like a sardine back there – the next time we go somewhere I refuse to travel No Frills! I –'

Her mouth gaped open as a pile of luggage came tumbling down the carousel, followed by an equally battered Lauren and Sandy.

'You see that?' crowed her husband, for once in his life getting the last word. '*That's* no frills...'

He received a withering look from his wife as Lauren and Sandy jumped off the carousel and pushed their way past the startled passengers. As they made their way through the crowd, a horrible screeching sound behind them made them turn and look back.

The carousel had ground to a halt. Trapped in the portal, his body too large to fit through, was Atkins. He struggled to free himself and stared venomously after the two girls.

Lauren and Sandy grinned at each other and raced over to an adjoining baggage claim – the baggage claim for Michael's flight.

Lauren grabbed a surprised flight attendant by the arm. 'Has this flight arrived?' she asked anxiously. The attendant nodded.

Lauren and Sandy scanned the crowd. It was a typical airport throng: holidaymakers, businessmen, a group of obnoxious schoolchildren, and a party of returning servicemen embracing their families. It was all perfectly normal.

And then they saw him. Dressed in a blue jacket and carrying a small black briefcase he was slipping quietly and quickly through the crowds to the street outside.

Each girl's hearts skipped a beat. At last they had found Michael.

Chapter Eighteen

Lauren and Sandy began to follow Michael when seemingly out of nowhere two arms appeared and grabbed them by the waist, holding them back. It was Al and his friend Dale from the flight.

'Well, howdy, girls,' said Al. 'Where you been?'

Elbowing the two salesmen in the stomach, Lauren and Sandy wrenched themselves free and ran after Michael. Evil frowns crossed over the men's faces as, suddenly no longer drunk, they chased after the girls. As they did so, Atkins, finally freed from the carousel and pursued by half a dozen extremely irate passengers, thundered past them, pushing them out of the way and running after the girls.

Unaware of Atkins, Lauren and Sandy burst out of the terminal building, shouting after Michael at the top of their lungs. But Michael was just too far away to hear as he got into a battered old cab, which swiftly pulled away and sped off down the road.

Lauren and Sandy looked around despondently. It was as bad as New York: there was never a cab around when it really mattered. Sandy pointed out to Lauren a three-wheeled motorbike at the kerb. It belonged to a butch metermaid who was having a heated argument with a double-parked driver.

The girl's didn't have to say a word to each other but ran over and jumped on the bike. Sandy pushed down hard on the accelerator and they revved off down the road, leaving the metermaid cursing and shaking her fist after them.

Atkins arrived just in time to see the fugitives disappear down the road in a cloud of dust. He turned to the Weasel who had followed him panting out of the terminal building.

'Goddamn them!' he growled. 'Get me a chopper – fast!'

Chapter Nineteen

It was worse than being on the rollercoaster at the fair, thought Lauren as she clung on to Sandy for dear life. At least on the roller coaster she would be strapped in and reasonably safe.

But with Sandy driving it seemed not a question of if, but when they would fall off the motorbike and quite probably break their necks.

Sandy, on the other hand, was having the time of her life, burning up rubber and breaking the State speed limit. She weaved in and out of the slow-moving traffic, running red lights and narrowly avoiding pedestrians as she pursued Michael's cab through the city streets and finally out onto the desert highway.

The wind whipped Lauren and Sandy's hair and faces as they increased their speed on the straight stretch of road. In the distance they could just make out Michael's cab as it drove away off into the mountains.

'We'll catch up with him if it's the last thing we do!' cried an ecstatic Sandy. She pushed her foot even further down on the accelerator.

Behind her Lauren whimpered. If Sandy's madcap driving was any thing to go by, it *would* be the last thing they'd ever do . . .

The cab finally drew to a halt by a dillapidated pier beside a huge mountain lake. The area was deserted save for a few holiday cabins, now unoccupied as the season had come to an end.

Michael paid the driver and got out of the cab. Clutching the briefcase closely to his side he set off down the pier, entering the shabby boat house at the end.

Lauren and Sandy arrived just as the cab pulled away. Sandy helped a grateful Lauren off the bike and together they stumbled off down the pier after Michael.

When they got to the door of the boat house they paused, suddenly afraid.

'I can't believe it,' marvelled Lauren.

'He's in there,' said Sandy. 'He's actually in there . . .'

A pause and then: 'Are you scared?'

Lauren snorted contemptuously. 'Why should *I* be afraid?'

'Why don't you rush into his arms then?' Sandy asked pointedly.

'Why don't you?' Lauren countered skilfully.

Another pause. Their eyes met. In that instant a flash of understanding passed between them.

'It's a long way to come for bad news . . .' Sandy said finally.

'Yeah . . .' agreed Lauren. She took a compact out of her pocket and snapped it open. She started to inspect her face in the mirror and immediately wished she hadn't: she looked awful. How could she present herself to Michael looking like the Creature from the Black Lagoon?

Looking over Lauren's shoulder Sandy looked at her own reflection. 'Yuk!' she grimaced as she stared at her drawn and tired face and her dishevelled hair. 'Oh no!' she suddenly cried in horror. 'Christ.'

'What is it?' asked Lauren anxiously.

'I *would* be getting a zit!'

'Where?' Lauren asked with genuine sisterly concern. Sandy pointed to the side of her nose.

Lauren inspected more closely. 'There is nothing there!' she scoffed. 'You're worse than I am! At least you've got eyelashes!'

'What else do you want?' complained Sandy. 'You're a natural blonde, *and* you tan. You make me sick...'

'Natural?' laughed Lauren. 'You thought this was natural? My dear Sandy, you too can have this colour!'

'No shit?' Sandy said admiringly. 'It looks great!'

'It's just a rinse with a cellophane toner –' explained Lauren and then broke off. What were they doing? They were supposed to be rivals for the same man, not best friends swopping beauty tips!

Putting her hand on the doorknob she turned to Sandy, trying hard to avoid her eyes. 'Well, I'd say "good luck" but...'

'Skip it,' said Sandy. 'May the best... whatever...'

Taking a deep breath, Lauren turned the knob and opened the door.

Chapter Twenty

The inside of the boat house was packed to the rafters with all manner of fishing paraphernalia – broken boats, oars, rods and reels, piles of old junk. Standing at the open door at the opposite end of the room, looking thoughtfully out to sea, was Michael.

As the door creaked open he spun round and in one deft movement whipped a gun out of his jacket. He aimed it at the two figures standing in the doorway.

'Michael, no!'

'It's me!'

Michael took a step back in amazement as he recognised the two people he least expected to see in the whole world. He stood there stunned and speechless, staring at each of the girl's faces in turn.

After a tense moment, he chuckled with relief. Suddenly he yelped in pain as a bullet whizzed past him, knocking the gun out of his hand and sending it flying through the back door over the end of the pier.

Atkins and the Weasel burst through the door behind Lauren and Sandy. A second bullet grazed Michael's leg and he fell to the floor with a thud.

Atkins and the Weasel went carefully over to Michael

when *CLANG!* they joined him unconscious on the floor. Standing behind them were Lauren and Sandy, each holding in their hands a heavy oar. In their eagerness to get Michael, Atkins and the Weasel had completely ignored the two girls.

Satisfied that Atkins and his crony would be out cold for hours, the girls went over to Michael and bent down to him in concern.

'He's all right,' said Sandy thankfully. 'He bumped his head when he fell but he'll come round.'

'Let's get him out of here!'

With great difficulty Lauren and Sandy managed to carry Michael's unconscious body away from the boat house and to the relative security of a secluded rocky overhang by the lakeside.

It was night time before he came round. He opened his eyes woozily and then shot up into a sitting position as he took in the sight of the two women who were crouched over him.

'Oh my God!' he cried in horror.

Sandy tried to hush him. 'Relax,' she whispered. 'It's only a bump.'

She smiled lovingly into his deep, deep blue eyes – and then realised that next to her Lauren was doing exactly the same. Once again the girls looked spitefully at each other and then turned back to Michael.

'Michael, I really think you owe us an explanation,' began Lauren. 'What exactly is your relationship with this woman?'

'Did you make it with her?' asked Sandy.

Michael looked from one girl to the other. '*That's* why you're here?' he asked incredulously.

'Well, I know you're in some sort of trouble,' Lauren

said sympathetically; 'but I'd like to discuss this first if you don't mind –'

'Right now,' reiterated Sandy.

Michael tried to understand. 'You did this on your own? There's no one with you?'

'He's changing the subject!' Sandy cried out, turning to Lauren. 'You see how he did that?'

'There's an issue here, Michael, that – I'm sorry – you're not going to get out of –'

Michael interrupted Lauren in mid-sermon. 'How did you follow me here?' he demanded. His voice had suddenly taken on an unpleasant edge.

'Well... we knew you weren't dead at the morgue,' Lauren explained, taken aback by Michael's abruptness.

'And you told them...' Michael's deep, deep blue eyes narrowed. Suddenly he didn't seem quite as attractive as before.

'Of course we told them,' continued Lauren, by now thoroughly confused. 'Why wouldn't we tell them?'

Michael ignored her and cursed under his breath.

'Wait a minute,' said Sandy, putting two and two together. 'You mean, you *wanted* to be dead?'

Before Michael could answer, the three of them heard the unmistakable whir of a helicopter high above them. A powerful search beam swept along the lakeside and made its way towards them. All three dived under the shelter of the overhanging rocks.

'It would have been useful...' Michael said sarcastically in response to Sandy's question. He whipped a walkie-talkie out of his jacket pocket and snapped urgently into it: 'Russell, abort the rendezvous. They've choppers all over me. Get out of here. I'll meet you in Tres Crucas. Over.'

'Screw 'em!' a voice crackled through the walkie-talkie. 'You've got the stuff!'

'No!' insisted Michael. 'We don't have the advantage any more. I will meet you in Tres Crucas. Acknowledge!'

'You're the boss,' Russell said. 'Over and out!'

Michael returned the walkie-talkie to his pocket as Lauren and Sandy looked on.

'Are you... not a schoolteacher, Michael?' asked Lauren slowly. The only answer he gave was an enigmatic – and slightly chilling – smile.

'Mike, what's going on?' asked Sandy. 'What's in Tres Crucas?'

'I'm very sorry you heard that...'

'Who cares what I heard!' snapped Sandy. 'What was I to you?'

'What was I?' repeated Lauren.

Michael looked dispassionately from one woman to the other. 'Convenient... moderately enjoyable... largely forgettable,' he said emotionlessly.

Lauren and Sandy stared at him open-mouthed, scarcely believing what they were hearing. He smirked cruelly and continued: 'And a lesson to me not to leave any loose ends... I'm sorry...'

Like a rattlesnake he suddenly lunged at the women. Screaming, they dived out of the way as the moonlight caught the glint of the knife he had whipped out of his jacket pocket.

Lauren and Sandy ran for their lives along the lakeside. His progress only slightly hindered by his injured leg, Michael snarled and bounded after them.

The chase rapidly became a deadly game of hide-and-seek, as Lauren and Sandy darted behind and in between boulders, trying desperately to find somewhere to hide from the man they once loved and who was now set to kill them both. All the time they could hear in the distance the whir of the circling helicopter, its persistent whining tearing their already tattered nerves to shreds.

At last they found temporary refuge behind a huge clump of bush. In the darkness Michael appeared to have disappeared. Apart from the drone of the helicopter everything was quite still – as still as the grave.

'Son of a bitch,' whispered Sandy to no one in particular.

Lauren, who was in a state of semi-shock, turned tearfully to Sandy. 'Loose end,' she choked. 'That's all I am to him? A loose end?'

Sandy shook her companion back to reality. 'What're you worrying about your love life going to shit? *We are going to die!*'

Suddenly from apparently out of nowhere Michael pounced on them. Wrenching themselves free, the girls left their cover and moved out into the open once more. Michael had them in a corner. Their only possible escape would be diving into the lake and swimming for it. Up above, the helicopter continued its search, its beam of light scanning the entire area.

Sandy pointed up. 'Who are they?' she shouted to Lauren.

'I don't know – they're after Michael,' Lauren shouted back above the noise of the engine and the whirring blades.

In an instant Sandy clicked. 'Then they must be the good guys!'

They began to jump up and down, waving their arms and shouting for help. But the noise of the chopper drowned out their cries and Michael was quickly catching up with them.

'Get in the light!' cried Lauren. 'We have to get into the searchlight! He can't follow us or they'll see him!'

Lauren and Sandy dashed for the searchlight as it continued its sweep of the area. But just as they were about to jump into its path it would suddenly move away in the other direction, to the right, to the left, and then to the right again, forever just missing them. And all the time Michael was weaving in and out of the light, joining Lauren and Sandy in their macabre dance, waiting for the chance to strike.

With one final mad dash Lauren and Sandy ran for the light. As the beam swept over again, it caught the reflection of Sandy's large glass ear ornament. It swiftly returned to the girls, bathing them in a steady shaft of light. Just outside the spotlight Michael stood dead still, unable to move into the circle of light and attack the girls. The girls and Michael regarded each other with undisguised hate.

'Looks like these loose ends are gonna stay loose a little longer.' Sandy spat the words at him.

Michael scowled, but realised he had no choice. Seeing a rope ladder descend from the helicopter, he turned and ran, rapidly being swallowed up in the all-enveloping blackness.

Lauren gratefully grabbed the ladder and hauled herself up into the chopper. Sandy quickly followed her.

Two strong arms helped both of them into the helicopter. The girls paused to catch their breath and then looked up at the man who had saved them.

When they recognised his face, they had to gasp for breath once more.

'*Weldon?*' Lauren said incredulously.

Weldon, the friendly wimp from the acting class, smiled sheepishly and introduced his partner – a sinister man with a bandage around his head. He was glaring at Lauren and Sandy with cold resentment.

'I guess you know Mr Atkins . . .' Weldon said weakly.

The girls turned to leave the helicopter in panic before realising they were thirty feet above the ground. Weldon laid a reassuring hand on both their shoulders.

'It's all right,' he said softly. 'We're CIA.'

Lauren and Sandy's reaction was as if someone had just told them that Ronald Reagan had voted for the Democrats. Weldon – CIA? Who was he trying to kid?

Weldon blushed under their stares and smiled apologetically.

Chapter Twenty-One

The helicopter had taken Lauren and Sandy to a concrete bunker some distance outside the Albuquerque city limits. For over an hour they had been cooped up in a featureless conference room with only Weldon and Atkins for company. The older man fired a barrage of questions at them while by his side a tape machine recorded every word the girls said.

'Well, I'm *so* sorry,' raged Sandy. 'It was stupid of us. We jumped to the incredibly insane conclusion that those guys chasing us and killing people were the heavies.'

Atkins stared humourlessly at her and stood up. He clicked off the machine and removed the spool of recorded tape. 'Thank you for your statement,' he said icily and strode smartly out of the room.

'Thank you for your statement . . ' repeated Sandy after he had left the room. 'Is that it?'

'You don't think we're entitled to know what all this is about, Weldon?' asked Lauren.

Weldon avoided her eyes. 'Me, personally, yes I do but – excuse me,' he said as he picked up the ringing phone at his side.

'Section 112 here,' he said briskly, suddenly sounding not at all like the Weldon Lauren and Sandy had known in the acting class. 'No! Don't cut the Ambassador any slack, he's up to his neck in this . . . no, never mind, just let me talk to him.'

He laid the receiver down and picked up the other phone on the desk. Speaking to the party on the other line he launched into what to Lauren and Sandy sounded like a stream of very fluent Russian.

The girls gasped in astonishment. Weldon hung up and picked up the first phone again.

'Hi, General. The Ambassador's pretending he's never heard of Floratoxin, how about that?' There was a hard edge of scorn in his voice. 'You better send out a code 07400 with Section 114 on standby in case there have to be evacuations. Right . . .'

He hung up and turned back to Lauren and Sandy who had by now convinced themselves that they had suddenly fallen into an old episode of *Get Smart!* 'Sorry,' he said, sounding once more like the Weldon they knew and tolerated. 'Can I offer you ladies a coffee or a Coke or –'

'Weldon, this is no time to play the perfect host!' Lauren pointed out sharply. 'What the hell is going on!'

Weldon looked down at his desk. 'Uh . . . I'm not authorised to debrief you,' he explained lamely.

'You can't debrief *me*!' blasted back Lauren. 'After I saved you from being throttled in class! Weldon!'

Weldon looked up – and straight into Lauren's big blue eyes. He loosened his collar for more air; he couldn't refuse those innocent questioning eyes.

'Who is Michael Sanders?' Lauren asked more gently.

'He was one of our very best operatives – very high

clearance, access to everything,' he explained. 'Then we began to suspect he was a double agent – working for Korzenowski...'

Lauren stopped him, trying desperately to take in the information. 'Wait a minute... Korzenowski? Our teacher?'

Weldon nodded. 'Your teacher, I'm sorry to tell you, was a key undercover man for the Russians.'

Lauren laughed derisively. There were only a certain number of unbelievable things a person could take before her first drink of the day. 'Oh, *please*... the man has a reputation. He was the definitive Lear...'

'He's the definitive KGB,' Weldon continued. 'That's why I was in that class. I was supposed to keep an eye on him, see if he and Sanders were in contact.'

'And they were!' came in Sandy.

'That's right, but we still don't know how – I never saw them come within a mile of each other. But somehow Korzenowski hired him.'

'What did Michael do?' asked Lauren.

'Stole a prototype of an experimental virus called Floratoxin. It's an airborne defoliant. A few drops can destroy vegetation for hundreds of miles.'

'As in grass? Trees?'

'As in California... the wheat belt,' said Weldon. 'All he has to do is spill a few drops and then the wind will do the rest.'

Lauren and Sandy sat back, shocked into silence as they took in the horrible implications.

'I want fifty million dollars, Joe – in cash. And please don't insult me by marking it.'

Michael's voice came through crisply on Atkins's office phone. By his side the Weasel listened on to the conversation, occasionally wiping the sweat off his chief's brow.

'Michael, we talked to the Director,' Atkins spoke evenly and calmly into the phone, just as if he were conducting a deal with an old business partner. 'We'll take this off the record if you come back in now.'

'You've had me shoot a few too many people who did that, Joe. I think you'd better get the money.'

Atkins raised his free hand in frustration: he knew when he was beaten. 'All right,' he gave in. 'It'll take a few hours. Where are you?'

At the other end of the line Michael laughed and then *click!* he had hung up.

Atkins bit his lip. 'Shit!' he cursed and stormed out of the office.

Back in the conference room a deal of another sort was trying to be made.

Lauren and Sandy had been observing Weldon for some time as he spoke furiously into the two phones on his desk. He was barking orders down them in a variety of languages: English, Spanish, Russian, Chinese, and for all Lauren and Sandy could tell, quite possibly Eskimo as well.

Lauren shook her head. She was having a hard time adjusting to the idea of Weldon as some sort of secret agent. The sweet young guy in acting class was not exactly the stuff James Bonds were usually made of.

'Yeah, I guess dorky waters run deep,' agreed Sandy. She caught Weldon's attention and cleared her throat. This wasn't going to be exactly easy.

'Er . . . Weldon . . . we don't want to be a drag, like, in a national crisis and all that, but . . . can we go home now?'

'Don't be ridiculous!' shrieked Atkins as he and the

Weasel led Lauren and Sandy down a tunnel to a waiting black van. 'They're his accomplices! They're professionals!'

'No, sir!' protested Weldon. 'I believe them!'

Atkins regarded him with contempt annoyed at Weldon's apparent naivety. 'You believe a couple of two-bit actresses could have tracked down someone like Michael Sanders? It was a rendezvous! They helped him escape! I was there – remember!'

'That was before they knew, sir!'

'Yeah, what did we know?' said Sandy, adding her voice to the argument. 'He was just this guy we happened to be boffing!'

'Damn it!' said Lauren, outraged at Sandy's statement. '*I* do not boff! *I* have *never* boffed in my entire life!'

Sandy cringed with irritation. 'OK – "had sex with", "made love with" . . . is that white enough for you?'

Taken aback, Lauren nodded meekly.

'Sir, when you go over their story . . .' Weldon began.

'That is exactly what I intend to do in a nice underground cell at Fort Morgan until we get Sanders's whereabouts!'

'You want his whereabouts? He told us he was going to Tres Crucas, New Mexico,' Lauren offered helpfully.

Atkins smirked sarcastically. 'Now, that was just a little too easy, wasn't it?'

'But it's the truth!'

'Forget it,' said Atkins and ushered them roughly into the back of the waiting van. He and Weldon climbed in after them and the Weasel shut the door behind them. Going to the front of the van he indicated to the two drivers who had been waiting in the front to move off.

As the van rumbled away out of the CIA building and off down the road, Lauren and Sandy sat down despondently on a spare tyre at the back of the van. They continued to plead their innocence to Atkins.

'Look, I know you're mad about your head,' said Lauren, determining to sympathise with him. 'I understand that. But if you'd just identified yourself –'

'Oh I see – walk up to an enemy operative and hand them my card?' Atkins responded sarcastically.

Suddenly the van bumped to a halt. Cursing to himself, Atkins leant over to the partition dividing the driver's cab from the rest of the vehicle. He suddenly found the nasty end of a gun pointing directly between his eyes.

Weldon made to grab the gun but the driver turned around in his seat and trained another gun on him. Lauren and Sandy gasped as they recognised the two men as Dale and Al, the salesmen they'd met on the flight to Albuquerque.

Al motioned for Weldon and Atkins to put up their hands. As they complied, Dale produced a canister and sprayed a fine white powder into their faces. Instantly the two CIA agents passed out.

Grinning, Dale divested them of their guns and then turned back to the steering wheel. The van set off again.

As it sped off down the roadway, Al regarded the girls who were cowering at the back of the ban. The former merry twinkle in his eyes had disappeared to be replaced by a hard cruel glint.

'I hate to let a good customer get away,' he said and casually removed his wig and a false nose piece.

'Some of us who teach can also do,' he sneered. The Texan drawl had now turned into a familiar Eastern European accent.

Lauren and Sandy looked at each other in amazement and then back at 'Al'.

They were looking into the face of their acting teacher, Korzenowski.

Chapter Twenty-Two

The girls remained staring in stunned silence for several long moments. Was no one whom he seemed? First Michael, then Weldon and Atkins, and now their teacher. They looked apprehensively at Dale: if he had taken off a mask and revealed himself to be Sean Connery they wouldn't have been in the least bit surprised.

'Vasily is lazy,' Korzenowski said, gesturing at his companion. 'He speaks no English.'

'What do you want?' asked Lauren warily.

'Where is Michael Sanders?'

Lauren sighed. 'Tres Crucas, New Mexico,' she repeated for what seemed to be the hundredth time.

'The truth, please.'

'It *is* the truth,' she groaned in frustration.

'You should know! You're the one he's working for!' argued Sandy. As she did so, she let her hand slip down behind the tyre she was sitting on. Her fingers alighted on a heavy metal jack.

'This is the last time I will ask you,' said Korzenowski and then recoiled automatically as Sandy threw the jack at his face. With lightning reflexes he raised his arm, deflecting the jack which landed with a sickening *thunk!* on Vasily's head. The Russian immediately slumped out cold over the steering wheel.

The van began to skid wildly all over the road. Forgetting Lauren and Sandy, Korzenowski shoved Vasily away from the steering wheel and tried to control the van as it shot off the road.

In the back of the van Lauren and Sandy were knocked from one side to the other as Lauren tugged down on the door handle, trying desperately to escape.

The van ploughed through a thicket of bushes until with a mighty crash it drove straight into a tree and stopped dead.

Lauren and Sandy looked over at Korzenowski. His head had hit the windscreen on impact and he seemed to be unconscious. With one final tug Lauren pulled down the door handle and pushed open the door. She leapt out of the van and started running for the cover of the trees.

Sandy began to follow her and then stopped still. Against her neck she felt the cold touch of a gun.

'I think you stay,' said Korzenowski who had quickly recovered from his stunned state.

Getting out of the passenger door, he moved round to the back of the van and spotted Lauren who was running towards a thicket of trees.

Calmly he raised the gun, took careful aim and fired.

Sandy screamed as Lauren suddenly fell lifeless to the ground. Korzenowski had done it: the bastard had actually killed her!

Korzenowski cooly replaced the gun in the shoulder holster beneath his jacket and marched over to Lauren's body. He regarded it dispassionately and nudged it with his foot. Bending down, he took her limp wrist in one hand while with the other he felt for a pulse.

In less than a second Lauren had grabbed his right hand and her other hand shot into his jacket, snatching his gun. In the next second Lauren was poking the gun hard in Korzenowski's ribs.

Lauren smiled with malicious pleasure. 'Was *that* death scene good enough for you, teach?' she asked with obvious relish.

The great man's face went white as Lauren continued mercilessly, eking out every bit of sadistic satisfaction she could find in her teacher's discomfort. 'Up! Up now!' she ordered. Slowly, they both rose to their feet, as an overjoyed Sandy came running up to them.

'We can make a bargain,' whimpered Korzenowski. 'The KGB is very generous!'

But Lauren wasn't interested. She prodded the gun even further into Korzenowski's rib cage, making him wince with pain. 'The KGB! Who cares about them? How dare you defraud the entire New York theatre community?'

'Lauren, this isn't the hot issue here,' Sandy reminded her.

Lauren nodded. 'OK, then, fine. You are going to tell us exactly what was going on it that class or . . . or . . .' – she handed Sandy the gun – '. . . or Sandy will shoot you.'

Sandy trained the gun on Korzenowski's lower anatomy. 'I'll shoot it off, Stan,' she said sadistically, enjoying every second.

Korzenowski looked down below his waist and then up at Sandy's gloating face.

He was suddenly very, very worried.

'We needed couriers,' he confessed.

'Between you and Michael,' Lauren completed his sentence. 'And we were the couriers?'

'It was nothing personal,' insisted Korzenowski. 'We were watched so closely.'

Sandy jabbed him in the ribs with the point of the gun. 'How?' she wanted to know.

'Your notebooks – I left microdots for him in yours,' he said to Sandy, and then turned to Lauren. 'He sent back his reply in yours.'

Lauren and Sandy's eyes narrowed. 'If he stole the toxin for you,' said Lauren, 'why don't you have it?'

Korzenowski burst out with a string of Russian expletives. Sandy got the point instantly. 'Hah! He screwed you too! The double-crossing, no-good son-of-a-bitch!'

However threatening Korzenowski and Atkins might originally have looked to Lauren and Sandy, they now appeared totally ridiculous as they sat tied to a tree trunk with the jump leads from the van. To add the final humiliation Lauren had just finished tying their hands together with her pantyhose. Nearby Weldon and Vasily were similarly tied to another tree trunk.

Korzenowski appeared particularly ludicrous, as he looked up from his sitting position at Lauren and Sandy, promising them all manner of favours if they would release him. 'I promise you,' he said. 'Help me now and we will be *very* generous.'

Lauren turned coldly on him. 'Are you suggesting that we'd be traitors?'

Korzenowski grunted non-commitedly.

'Hey, I might cheat the phone company,' Sandy said indignantly, 'but I do not betray the United States of America! Is that clear, Jack?' she said, turning to Atkins.

'All right, obviously I made a mistake,' he said sulkily. 'But if you'll just put yourselves in my hands you'll walk away from this right now with full federal protection . . .'

Lauren and Sandy pretended to consider the proposal, but secretly were enjoying the way the tables had been totally overturned.

'Do you think he means it?' Lauren asked Sandy.

Behind Atkins's back, Weldon furiously shook his head, confirming the girls' suspicions.

'We will set up the most discreet trust fund,' promised Korzenowski. 'One million dollars tax free.'

'We'll guarantee complete immunity from conspiracy charges,' countered Atkins, '*and* reimbursement for all expenses . . .'

Sandy had had enough. 'Oh, stop it! You are both so full of it! C'mon, Lauren, let's get out of here!'

Lauren nodded, but first walked over to the bound Weldon. 'Thanks for trying, Weldon,' she said and bent down to kiss him on the cheek. He instantly turned bright red.

'I . . . I . . . I . . .' he stammered.

'Save it, Weldon,' Lauren said, and followed Sandy. Within minutes they had disappeared into the trees.

'We'll find you!' Atkins called after them.

'Yeah, you do that!' Sandy's voice came back like a challenge.

For several minutes the four men sat there in silence. Atkins and Korzenowski were fuming, shamed at being defeated by two actresses.

Finally Atkins turned to Korzenowski with a sign. 'Well, Stan,' he began, just as if he were talking to a long-lost buddy, 'I guess you're looking at a KGB tribunal . . .'

Korzenowski looked suspiciously at his rival, catching the tone in his voice.

'. . . unless, of course, you'd rather make other arrangements?' finished Atkins.

‘Would such “arrangements” include an expense account ... condo on the Potomac ... Redskin season tickets?’ the Russian asked eagerly.

Atkins smiled. ‘Welcome aboard, Stan! Welcome aboard!’

Chapter Twenty-Three

Feeling like extras from a 1960s 'road' movie, Lauren and Sandy stood on the edge of the dusty dirt road leading down to Tres Crucas. Sandy was holding her thumb out, hoping to hitch a lift. The one problem with her technique was that there wasn't a car in sight.

'Well,' sighed Lauren. 'I guess we're really a couple of chumps.'

Sandy chuckled self-effacingly, wondering how Michael could have fooled her for so long. 'God, I really should've seen it, you know. Notebooks! He hit on us for our goddamn notebooks!'

'Hit on! He made me pick him up!'

Sandy smiled. 'I attacked him in a Burger King!'

'I stayed up all night to work on this FUCKING PUMPKIN COSTUME for one of his mythical students!' Lauren marvelled at her own naivety.

'Hey, I baked cookies for his whole class! I mean, can you see me baking – at a stove! With an apron! Icing those gross little happy faces on every fucking one of them!'

Lauren considered the image and broke out laughing.

'I got thirty thank-you notes!' continued Sandy.

'In crayon?' giggled Lauren.

'Yeah!' said Sandy who was laughing now too. It was good to share a joke again.

'I paid five thousand dollars to study with the KGB!' Lauren was now almost hysterical and tears of laughter were streaming down her face.

'Hey, he thrashed me worse than you!' Sandy reminded her. 'Hamlet! I ask you, how am *I* gonna know Hamlet?'

'You should if you're an actress,' Lauren pointed out gently.

'Well, pardon me!' Lauren had hit a raw nerve. 'We can't all go to the London School of Shakespearean Weirdness! Some of us had to schlepp Big Macs for a living!'

'I'm . . . I'm sorry . . .' said Lauren. She meant it – and Sandy knew it.

'Forget it.' Sandy waved the criticism aside. 'Where're we going to go now?' she asked.

'I don't know. They'll be after us soon . . . but I was thinking . . .'

'Yeah,' said Sandy wistfully. 'So was I . . .'

'What?'

'That we go find Michael and rip his face off?' she asked eagerly.

'That – and get the toxin.'

'To hell with the toxin!' cried Sandy, determined to get her priorities right. 'I want to rip his face off!'

'No, we need the toxin,' stressed Lauren, finding herself for once in the unusual situation of being the practical one. 'We can't have the CIA after us for the rest of our lives! And what if he spills the stuff? We can't let him do that.'

Sandy considered the matter. She supposed Lauren

was right. 'OK – as long as we still get to rip his face off.'

'I promise you we'll rip his face off!' said Lauren, relishing the bloody prospect as much as Sandy.

Sandy smiled. 'So what are we waiting for?' she said. 'You're the one with the legs – go get us a lift!'

Tres Crucas was not the sort of place that anyone would miss in a nuclear war. With a population of 142 the cacti outnumbered the people by thousands to one.

The streets were simply paths where the mud wasn't quite so thick, and along which pigs seemed to have the right of way. Indians and Mexicans shuffled along, each minding their own business and muttering away to themselves. Occasionally a hippie would pass by in kaftan and beads – over forty and still dreaming of Woodstock.

As the huge oil truck in which they had hitched a lift rumbled off into the distance, Lauren and Sandy turned up their noses in disgust. The place reeked of bad sanitation.

'Well, what'll we do first?' Lauren asked. 'Get a little sushi and take in a show?'

Sandy glared at her. 'Whose bright idea was this?'

'Ours,' Lauren reminded her.

'I know, I know,' groaned Sandy. 'But I'm so tired and dirty and –' She looked up at the scorching sun overhead. 'And I am not a day person!'

Suddenly Lauren and Sandy found themselves having to leap to the edge of the dirt track as a huge truck filled with leering Mexican labourers sped past, spattering them with mud and dust. As it passed them, the Mexicans shouted to them in Spanish: it was patently obvious what they were suggesting.

'Now, why do they do that?' Lauren asked after they

had gone. 'Do you think there's even been one woman in the history of the world who said "yeah, fellas, take me now!"?'

'For a bed and a bath I'd consider it...' Sandy said seriously.

Before Lauren could protest they were approached by one of the town's hippy contingent. He wasn't unattractive in a Beau Bridges sort of way, and was wearing a dirty cheesecloth shirt and a pair of tattered old blue jeans. He was the sort of guy who had come to the Southwest in the sixties to live off the land and soon discovered that he could live a lot better off the tourists. Sandy thought he looked like the kind of person who still thought Bob Dylan was pretty cool.

'You're looking for a guide, right?' He launched into his standard spiel. 'A native Indian to show you the hidden wonders of this great Chicatacawa nation?' Lauren and Sandy shook their heads emphatically, but he didn't seem to notice. 'You got him. Twenty bucks.' He held out his hand.

Sandy looked him up and down. 'I don't want to be the first one to break this to you, but you are *not* an Indian!'

The hippie looked hurt. 'Hey, that's a technicality! An accident of birth! I've been a full member of the Chicatacawa tribe since '68!'

'Look, I'm sure you're a colourful local character,' Lauren began charitably, 'but what we really need right now is a man –'

The hippie sighed. 'All right, it's not gonna be that great though – I'm pretty bombed...'

'No!' Lauren said quickly.

'Twenty dollars?' he asked hopefully.

'No. We're looking for a specific person.'

'Oh – then you want a tracker!'

Lauren and Sandy exchanged blank glances.

'A guy who tracks down other guys,' he explained.

Lauren nodded. She was with him now. George at the Institute was something like that.

'You wanna find this guy?' continued the hippy. 'I'll hunt him like a dog.'

Lauren and Sandy looked doubtful.

'Ancient Chicaw technique... listening to the ground... the whole hog,' he said, and produced a business card from his shirt pocket.

Sandy read it aloud: '*Frank Madras: Licensed Tracker; Psychic; Fiat Repair*... Oh, please!'

'Ah, c'mon,' said Frank, almost pleading. 'How many trackers do you meet?'

'Not very many with gold chains,' admitted Lauren, pointing to the expensive jewellery around Frank's neck.

Frank looked even more hurt and buttoned up his shirt in embarrassment. 'Look, you wanna find this guy or not?'

Lauren and Sandy felt like they were in an episode of *The Big Valley*. Frank was leading them around in circles, every so often sniffing the air, or diving to his knees and pressing an ear to the ground. Lauren half-expected him to do a rain dance; Sandy was idly wondering just when Barbara Stanwyck would appear on the scene.

Suddenly Frank leapt to his feet, stiffened and sniffed the air once more. 'He passed this way,' he announced confidently.

'How on Earth can you know that?' asked Lauren, not convinced.

Frank sniffed again. 'Super unleaded,' he explained. 'No one around here can afford it.'

Sandy shook her head in despair. 'Let's dump this gerkhin,' she suggested to Lauren.

'Hey, c'mon!' protested Frank. 'Like, I can relate to your problem here! I used to be white myself!'

Lauren and Sandy looked him up and down. Frank had definitely been out in the desert for far too long. The hot sun had finally got to him.

'How exactly did you become an Indian?' Lauren asked, humouring him.

'Made the Top Ten with my draft card back in '66,' Frank said. 'Canada was too cold, so I came down here. These guys found me out in the desert one night, flat on my back, freezing my ass off, trying to burn a dollar. We've been blood brothers ever since . . .'

Frank pointed to a rundown cantina, some way down the road. 'That's it,' he said.

'Michael's in there?' Lauren couldn't believe it: Michael might be a traitor and a louse but even he wouldn't frequent a dump like that.

Frank showed her the set of footprints in the dirt leading up to the hotel.

'Those could be anybody's!' scoffed Sandy.

Frank nodded sagely. 'Yeah, they could be anybody's – anybody about 185 pounds, dragging his right foot a little like he was injured.' He bent down to pick up a cigarette butt from the ground and sniffed at it. 'And he smokes hand-rolled Colton's every three minutes . . .'

Lauren and Sandy stared at Frank with grudging respect, as he smiled proudly back at them. 'Ancient Indian technique,' he told them. 'Admit it, this man is cool.'

'OK, OK, don't rub it in,' said Sandy and opened the door of the cantina. The interior of the bar was almost as bad as its outside appearance. Gangs of grubby unshaven ranchers hung about the counter, putting back straight shots of tequila and seeming as if they were looking for a fight.

A boozy Mexican and a fat middle-aged woman were dancing on the small dance floor to the loud Mexican music which blared from a dilapidated juke box in the corner. As the girls and Frank entered the bar, the bartender stormed out from behind his counter.

'Madras, you son of a bitch!' he bellowed. 'Pay your tab!'

Frank smiled weakly at the two girls. 'Ancient Chacatacawa greeting,' he explained.

As Frank tried to bargain with the bartender, Lauren and Sandy moved nervously further into the bar. Almost instantly they were approached by two roughnecks who grinned lustfully at them.

'That dirty hippie ain't a fittin' date for you, honey,' one of them said to Sandy.

Sandy sighed. Disaster, or at the very least attempted rape, was imminent. With a flash of sudden inspiration she put her arm possessively around Lauren. 'Hey, who says I'm with him?' she asked. 'I'm with her. Ain't that right, baby?' She gave Lauren a proprietary peck on the lips.

Quickly catching on, Lauren gazed lovingly into Sandy's eyes. 'Listen,' she whispered. 'They're playing our song.' With a flamboyant sweep she led Sandy out onto the dance floor.

Totally deflated, the two roughnecks wandered back to their places at the bar, muttering about 'goddamn dykes'.

Lauren and Sandy gracefully danced their way across the dance floor and back to Frank who had somehow managed to placate the bartender *and* appropriate a bottle of whisky. Sandy noticed that the gold chain around his neck had disappeared.

'All right,' demanded Lauren. 'Where's Michael?'

'He's probably upstairs,' Frank answered, pointing to the staircase at the back of the bar.

'What's upstairs?' asked Sandy.

Frank sighed. Now, how was he going to explain this one to them?

Chapter Twenty-Four

The closest Lauren had ever been to a 'house of pleasure' before was watching *The Best Little Whorehouse in Texas* on TV. And the sight which greeted her eyes as she climbed the stairs was as far removed from Miss Parton's 'piddlin' little country place' as *I, Claudius* was from a children's tea party. Even Sandy's mouth gaped open in astonishment as she peeped her head around a discreetly placed partition to take a look.

The stairs led directly up to a landing which had been turned into a lusciously decorated reception room. On velvet sofas, customers in various states of undress sat with scantily-clad women who were toying and teasing with them. Other girls wearing only garter belts, stockings and the tiniest of chemises lolled around smoking cigarettes. Occasionally one of the girls would lead a customer down the hall and into one of the adjoining bedrooms. The air was heavy with the irresistible scent of decadence, divine or otherwise.

Presiding over the affair was a fat blowsy madam, looking like a Mae West gone to seed. Dolly Parton she most definitely was not.

'Wow,' whispered Sandy behind the partition which

screened her, Lauren and Frank from view. 'This is some major ill reupte happening here.'

'Now, wait a minute,' Lauren said. 'Michael wouldn't stop in the middle of everything that's at stake here and patronise a . . . a . . . sleazy cathouse . . . would he?' She sounded doubtful. After all, when a guy's double-crossed, lied, cheated, stolen, attempted to kill you, betrayed his country and was even now considering destroying that country's food crops, why should he worry too much over spending one night of naughtiness here and there?

'Sure he would,' said Frank. 'It's the only hotel for a hundred miles.'

'So what's this?' Sandy said, looking at the whores. 'Room service?'

Lauren and Sandy began to move away from the cover of the partition but Frank pulled them back. 'No way,' he said firmly. 'It's customers only.'

Lauren and Sandy glanced over to the madam. Nothing short of a ten ton tank would get past her.

'Customers . . .' Sandy repeated and thoughtfully stroked her chin. She looked over to Lauren and both girls turned their gaze to Frank. There was a wicked gleam in their eyes.

'Get the shirt,' said Lauren. 'I'll get his hat and pants.'

'Hey, you had your chance before!' protested Frank.

'Don't get too excited,' Sandy said. 'We don't want your body.' Frank's face fell. 'Just your clothes.' Frank's face fell even more.

Slowly the two women closed on him. Frank didn't stand a chance.

The madam eyed the two boys standing before her with suspicion. Their smooth faces were almost girlish and their slight builds were emphasised by Frank's oversized clothes. Each of them was wearing a cowboy hat, into which 'he' had tucked 'his' long hair.

They stood twitching under her critical stare, shifting from foot to foot, refusing to meet her eyes.

'Who are you kidding?' she said finally. 'How old are you boys? Thirteen? Fourteen? You don't even shave yet! Your father know you're here?'

Lauren and Sandy looked at each other and then back down at the floor, mumbling what they considered to be their best prepubescent mumble. The madam nodded knowingly.

'Ohhhhh, I see,' she said kindly. 'First time?'

'No way!' cried Lauren in what she hoped was a convincing voice. She pointed accusingly at Sandy. 'It's *his* first time!'

'You wish!' Sandy belted back.

'You chickenshit, huh?'

'I'm not chickenshit!'

'He's chickenshitting out!'

'I'm not!' protested Sandy and pushed Lauren back. Lauren defended herself and soon they were involved in a boyish tussle.

The madam looked on in amusement and then clicked her fingers. Lauren and Sandy stopped their fight and looked up to see two busty and fearsome-looking whores standing before them. They were dressed in scanty red chemises and long black stockings and stilettos.

'This is Tina and Marie.' The madam winked at the two 'boys'. 'Have fun.'

Lauren and Sandy gulped as the two whores took them down the corridor and up the stairs to the second floor. As they followed on reluctantly, Lauren turned miserably to Sandy. 'I'm *upset* about this!' It was the understatement of the year.

'Hey, relax, maybe you'll learn something,' quipped Sandy and then, seeing Lauren's hurt expression, hastily added: 'Just kidding. Come on.'

The whores were too bored to look behind them to see if Lauren and Sandy were following. If they had done they would have seen Lauren stopping at each closed door, sniffing like a bloodhound, and then carrying on.

'What are you doing?' asked Sandy.

'I'm smelling,' was the obvious reply. Sandy wondered whether the events of the past few days had finally proved too much for Lauren and said so.

'I'm smelling for tobacco smoke,' Lauren retorted indignantly.

'That's stupid,' said Sandy. 'We're not gonna –' She stopped in her tracks, struck by a certain smell. Lauren too had detected the faint but unmistakable aroma of Michael's Colton's tobacco.

'All right, Sherlock Holmes,' Sandy said pointing to the door behind which they could smell the tobacco, 'he's in there. What if he's awake?'

Lauren shook her head. 'If he's lit a cigarette then they've already done it.'

Sandy remembered. 'Then he's out cold!'

'Did you ever think you'd be glad men roll over and pass out?' Lauren reached for the door knob. Down the corridor the two whores plodded on, unaware that they had just lost two of their strangest customers ever.

The only furniture in the room was a chair and a primitive bedstead above which on the wall there hung an ornamental goat's head. Michael was asleep. Sitting by him on the bed was a pretty Oriental girl who was putting on her stockings.

She looked up when the girls came in, only slightly surprised at the intrusion. They put their fingers to their lips, motioning for her to remain quiet. She shrugged indifferently and continued to roll up her stockings.

Lauren tiptoed over to Michael's jacket which was hanging from a chair and took out his wallet. Extracting several bank notes from it she handed them to the girl who took the hint, as well as the money, and left the room, leaving Lauren and Sandy alone with Michael. Lauren and Sandy took off their hats and shook free their long hair.

Lauren regarded Michael thoughtfully for several seconds: his gorgeous square-jawed good looks, his full chest, his strong biceps, the look of little boy contentment on his face.

Turning to Sandy she said softly: 'You know, I've come to a definite decision.'

'What's that?'

'You can have him.'

Sandy grinned and approached the bed, flexing her fingers. There was murder in her eyes. 'Where's a chainsaw when you need one?' she asked viciously.

Lauren caught her arm before she could do anything which might land her in court on a charge of justifiable homicide. 'Sandy,' she said soothingly, 'I'm mad too but right now raking him with our fingernails is not in our best interests. OK?'

Sandy looked disappointed at being cheated out of a little fun, but nodded in agreement.

'Just keep an eye on him while I go through his clothes,' said Lauren and went over to the chair.

Just then Michael groaned in his sleep and rolled over, feeling for the Oriental girl who had been by his side. Lauren and Sandy exchanged a look of panic.

Quickly Sandy went over and got into the bed beside Michael, who put his arm around her. Sandy gritted her teeth in revulsion as Michael once more fell back into a deep sleep.

Lauren, meanwhile, was searching frantically through Michael's pockets until she found what she was looking for in a secret pouch in the jacket's lining. She pulled out a small plastic packet and opened it up. Inside was a small sealed vial filled with a colourless liquid. She showed the vial triumphantly to Sandy and then replaced the vial back into the packet, shutting it with a *snap!*

Michael's eyes popped open at the sound. They widened even more when he found himself staring straight into Sandy's face.

Sandy smiled her most brilliant smile. 'Was it good for you too?' she asked sweetly and in one quick movement brought the goat's head above the bed crashing down onto Michael's head.

Leaping out of bed, she threw the covers over his face and dashed out of the bedroom, following Lauren who clutched the packet containing the vial in her hand.

Like a couple of football pros they bludgeoned their way past the whores and their clients in the reception room. Michael stumbled after them, desperately trying to put on his pants at the same time.

The girls thundered down the stairs, through the crowd at the bar and out into the street. Moments later Michael bounded down the stairs in hot pursuit.

'Hey, brother, you're wasting your time with those two,' a roughneck said resentfully as Michael raced on past him.

Out in the street the same pick-up truck that had passed Lauren and Sandy before was about to move off.

Seeing the two girls, the Mexicans jeered loudly at them.

'Hey, babes! *Mamacitas?* Wanna ride?'

'Yes? Yesyesyesyes!' cried the girls, leaping onto the back of the truck.

'You guys are the sweetest, most gorgeous creatures in the whole wide world!' Lauren gave the nearest Mexican a big sloppy kiss on the cheek.

The Mexicans stared at each other, paralysed with shyness and shock. Not quite knowing what to do now that their wildest dreams had been realised, they raised their hats deferentially to the two girls.

Lauren and Sandy looked back anxiously to the cantina and saw Michael burst through the door. There was a knife in his hands.

Sandy shouted across to the driver in the cab of the truck.

'*Andele! Andele,* James!'

The driver pressed his foot hard down on the accelerator and the truck sped off down the road, leaving Michael standing alone in a cloud of dust, cursing and waving his fist angrily after them.

From the back of the truck Lauren and Sandy waved mockingly back.

Chapter Twenty-Five

After half an hour the Mexican truck driver drew to a halt in the middle of nowhere. Lauren looked anxiously at him. 'Why did we stop?' she asked, fearing the worst.

'*No hablo Inglese*,' was the answer.

'Look, we have to get to a phone,' pleaded Sandy.

But it was no use. The Mexicans were all jumping off the back of the truck and unloading shovels. With a single-mindedness of purpose, they set about digging.

Sandy and Lauren looked on in despair, and then gasped as the last Mexican got off. Hidden up to now in the corner of the truck and dressed in a weird combination of clothes taken from Lauren and Sandy's wardrobe was Frank. He looked very much pissed off.

'What are *you* doing here?'

Frank looked down bitterly at the clothes he had been forced to exchange with Lauren and Sandy in the whorehouse. 'Getting a ride back to the reservation before one of those guys asks for my phone number!'

'C'mon, you look kinda cute,' Sandy called after him as he jumped off and began heading off across the sand.

'Yeah,' agreed Lauren. 'And that skirt never suited me.'

'Hang on a minute,' Sandy said urgently. 'Did he say phone?'

Lauren looked at her. 'I think he did!' Leaping off the truck they began walking briskly after Frank who was already some twenty yards ahead. He looked behind nervously and increased his pace. The girls increased theirs. Finally he broke into a run; the girls did similarly.

It is not the easiest thing in the world for a two hundred pound man in high heels and a skirt to outrun two desperate females. With a tackle that the San Francisco Forty-Niners would have been proud of, Lauren and Sandy brought Frank down to the ground with a sickening *thud!*

'Sorry, Frank, it's important,' apologised Lauren as she and Sandy held him struggling down to the ground.

'Get away! Get away from me!' he cried.

'Look, Frank,' pleaded Sandy. 'We gotta use your phone!'

'Forget it! You stiff me twenty bucks, you leave me in drag, you got some freak with a knife after you,' he barked. 'These things do not exactly inspire me to buddy up you babes!' Overcome by his outburst he raised his hand to his temple. 'Ow – what's wrong with my head?'

'Are you okay?' asked Sandy.

Frank glowered at her. 'No,' he said ruefully. 'I'm sober.'

Sandy grabbed him by the shoulders and looked him straight in the eyes. 'Listen – we're not jerking you around. Some men are chasing us because one of them stole a virus. It'll destroy all the trees and plants for hundreds of miles, but now we stole it back so now they want to kill us!'

Frank stared in amazement, scarcely comprehending. 'Jesus! The sixties were good to you, weren't they?'

'Yes, Frank, think back to the sixties!' Lauren interjected. 'People did things for each other then – they cared about each other!'

'They were wasted,' he moaned, ignoring Lauren's appeal.

'There's a reward,' Lauren added. Frank's eyes lit up.

Lauren took Sandy aside. 'Don't tell him that!' she admonished in a stage whisper. 'A hundred thousand split three ways is nothing!'

Sandy tried to look convincing. 'We have no choice,' she said and turned back to an eager Frank. 'If you help us get to a telephone I swear to you you will be showered with money.'

Frank looked slowly from one woman to the other. He sighed. 'I'm gonna regret this . . .' he said, resigned.

The hot desert sun blazed mercilessly down on Lauren, Sandy and Frank as they tramped on through the sand now wearing their own clothes. Except for a few cacti, there was nothing to be seen for miles. Occasionally they would hear the distant howl of a coyote but other than that the only thing which broke the oppressive silence were Lauren and Sandy's periodic grumbles.

'How many miles till we get to something – anything?' asked Sandy wearily.

Frank shrugged. 'Fifty-two Chictaw kayakas . . . That's about eleven miles.'

'Great,' muttered Sandy. 'Nothing to do for eleven miles . . .'

'So, anyway,' Sandy began shyly as they trudged further on. 'What's *Hamlet* about anyway?'

Lauren smiled. 'Well, Hamlet was a guy who wanted revenge.'

'That's it?'

'More or less.'

'Yeah . . .' mused Sandy. 'That I can relate to.'

'Sure you can. It's just Shakespeare. It won't bite you.'

'I thought it was all, you know, people standing around in togas . . .'

'Oh no! There's a ghost – murder and lust, greed and adultery . . .'

'Wow!' Sandy was impressed. It sounded better than *Dynasty*.

'And great, great language,' enthused Lauren and quoted: 'To suffer the slings and arrows of outrageous fortune.'

'Yeah . . .' said Sandy, struck by the beauty of the words. 'What does it mean?'

'Kind of like the last two days . . .'

Further on into the trek Sandy had become really interested in the story of the Prince of Denmark.

'So what happens after he dumps Ophelia?' she asked Lauren.

'She drowns herself,' answered Lauren.

'Men are pigs,' Sandy said with feeling.

Chapter Twenty-Six

'This is it?' asked Sandy, decidedly unimpressed.

Frank had led them out of the desert to a tumbledown medium-sized tourist shack which seemed as if it had last done service in a second-rate Spaghetti Western. Above the door which was leaning off its hinges there hung a crooked sign on which were scrawled the words:

FRANK'S TRADING POST
Authentic Indian Relics
Ash Trays – Sacred Rocks – Yucca Candy
Live Gila Monsters

For miles around they could see nothing but the vast expanse of sand and rocks and the seemingly ubiquitous cacti.

'Not exactly the hub of the reservation, is it?' Lauren remarked.

Frank was offended. 'Hey! It's off-season! What do you expect?'

He opened the door and as they crossed the threshold he warned them: 'Five minutes, that's all you've got. If you stay here more than five minutes you'll bring a goddamn tornado down on us, I know it!'

'Frank, we have no intention of hanging around,' Lauren promised him and looked around the tourist shack. 'The sooner we get out of here and on our way the –'

She suddenly broke off and grabbed Sandy's arm. Sandy followed her pointing finger past the postcard stands and the tacky Indian souvenirs until she saw what had so captured Lauren's attention.

'I *want* that blouse!' Lauren said definitely.

As Frank watched on in pure masculine amazement Lauren and Sandy pushed their way past the gaudy souvenir stands to a rack of prairie blouses. Sandy grabbed a bright orange one.

'This is my colour,' she declared, holding it up to her chest and preening herself in the full-length mirror.

'I wore one of these when I was in *Oklahoma*,' Lauren said as she tried on one of the blouses.

Sandy looked on appreciatively. 'That's cute on you.'

'You don't think it makes me short-waisted?'

'Nah,' said Sandy. 'Get a snakeskin belt and you'll get a little texture going... Say, what do you think of this one?'

'Take them! Take them!' Frank exploded, losing his patience. 'The blouses are on the house!' He grabbed the phone from off the wall and handed it to Lauren. 'Now, I hate to bring this up but you guys did say you wanted to use my phone, like it was a national emergency and all that.'

'OK, all right!' said Lauren. 'Who do we call? *The New York Times?* No! We'll call the President!'

'Oh, sure he'll take that call,' mocked Sandy. 'Hi – we're two struggling actresses and we've saving the world.'

Lauren silenced Sandy's sarcasm. 'All right then, we'll

call the FBI. We've got to turn this in –' She took the toxin out of her pocket as Sandy jiggled with the receiver.

'Damn it! It doesn't work!'

'They must have cut me off,' said Frank. 'I owe them a little money...'

Sandy looked at him in despair. 'Don't you know how to handle these dorks? You don't *have* to pay them!'

'You don't?' Frank was suddenly very interested.

'No, you just –'

'*Sandy!*'

'Whoops, sorry,' Sandy apologised to Lauren and then asked, 'How do we get to a phone that works, Frank?'

'No problem,' he replied blithely. 'Just follow me around the back...'

Lauren and Sandy looked doubtfully at the tired old horse who was tethered to a rail at the back of Frank's shack. The only horse Sandy had ever ridden was at the fairground when she was a kid. And Lauren was only used to riding thoroughbreds – certainly not a mangy old nag which should have gone to the knacker's yard years ago.

Oblivious to the girls' feelings Frank beamed with pride at the horse as he untied it from the rail.

'OK, ladies, this is Frodo,' he said introducing them to their transport. He gestured over to the horizon. 'You're going to cross those hills till you get to the edge of a cliff. Don't go off there, it's a seven hundred feet drop. Bear right and you'll come to a narrow path, down the side of the cliff – unless it's washed out in which case good luck...'

Lauren and Sandy's hearts sank but there was more: 'If you make it down you'll come to the rattlesnake area.

Be real careful in there. Go right at the rattlesnakes and take the dirt road till you get to the taco stand. You'll find a phone there.'

Sandy groaned. 'I might have known it wouldn't just be a block and a half to the corner store . . .' She turned to Lauren. 'How did that bit from *Hamlet* go again?' she asked.

'To suffer the slings and arrows of outrageous fortune.'

'Yeah, that . . . poor guy – I know just how he felt . . .'

'We won't forget you, Frank,' Lauren promised. 'We'll see you get something out of this.'

He waved his hand dismissively. He'd heard it all before. 'Yeah, I'll be showered with money. I can hardly wait,' he said wearily.

With all the enthusiasm of a comatose tortoise he helped Sandy onto Frodo. Lauren was about to climb on behind her when she felt her pocket. 'My God!' she cried. 'The toxin! I don't have it!'

Panicking, she ran back to the front of the shack. Rushing inside the shack she saw the packet containing the vial of toxin lying where she had left it on the table.

She snatched it up and turned to leave – to find Michael standing in the doorway blocking her way. He was pointing a gun at her head.

'Hand it to me,' he ordered. '*Very* slowly!'

Lauren was defiant. 'No. I won't do it.'

He cocked the gun. Lowering her head in defeat, Lauren slowly handed the toxin over to him. As she did so she made a desperate attempt to push past him through the door. Michael struck her viciously on the side of her head with his gun.

Round the back Sandy and Frank heard Lauren's scream. As Sandy started, Frank gave the horse a smart slap on its behind. Like a guided missile it darted off with Sandy holding on to the reins for dear life. It ran along the side of the shack, almost trampling the two armed hoods who were standing by Michael's parked jeep. They dived for cover as the horse and Sandy galloped off across the desert.

The men advanced menacingly on Frank who had come out from the back of the shack. With a lightning movement one of them struck him over the head with his gun. As Frank fell senseless to the ground Michael appeared out of the shack. He was carrying an unconscious Lauren in his arms.

He unceremoniously dumped her in the back of the jeep and glared down evilly at her as she came to.

'Now you're really going to make yourself useful,' he sneered.

Lauren shivered with fear as one of Michael's accomplices got in the jeep beside her and pointed his gun intimidatingly at her.

In Atkins's office the atmosphere was electric. When the telephone rang, Weldon and the agents who were huddled around the desk jumped with expectation.

Atkins slowly picked up the receiver and switched on the loudspeaker system so that everyone could hear the conversation.

'Hello, Joe.' It was Michael's voice. 'Do you have the money?'

'It's here.' By Atkins's side an agent opened up a leather briefcase: it was packed with stacks of thousand dollar bills.

'You will get a chopper and fly to Mesa Azul.' Atkins instructed Weldon to take down the details as Michael continued: 'Forget about ground support: I'll have lookouts and if we see one sniper or tank or plane or chopper other than your chopper, I'm going to drop the toxin right on the ground.'

Atkins and his men regarded each other in miserable silence.

'You will not bring the chopper down,' ordered Michael. 'You will stay level with the mesa and lower the money down to me at 1700 hours. Understand that?'

'No!' Atkins shouted down the receiver. 'That's totally unacceptable!'

Michael had hung up. Atkins turned to his men. 'It's all under control,' he said weakly, trying to save face. 'We know where he is, we can secure the area.'

His voice tailed off, as Weldon said, 'Uh, sir, the "area", as you call it, is two hundred square miles of thousand feet cliffs. There are no roads in or out. If I were choosing a ransom drop I'd be hard-pressed to find a better one.'

Atkins glared at Weldon. 'We've still got him,' he claimed. 'He can't outrun us.'

'Excuse me, sir,' Weldon pointed out. 'He grew up out there. One man on foot who knows that country can hide there indefinitely.'

Atkins buried his face in his hands. Weldon was absolutely right. It looked as though Michael had won after all.

Chapter Twenty-Seven

Frank came too with a splitting headache. Opening his eyes, he noticed with some surprise that he was lying face down in the dirt outside his shack, and not on a bar-room floor, which was the usual place he found himself when he woke up with a splitting headache. He put his hand tentatively to his temple: there was some congealed blood but otherwise he'd survived the hoods' vicious attack with a minimum of injury.

Groggily he lifted himself up out of the dirt and looked around. Silhouetted in the afternoon sun a horse and rider stood before him. As he peered more closely at the figure on the horse he realised that it was Sandy. Finally having given up any attempt to control Frodo, she had let the horse go where he had wanted to go – right back to Frank.

Frank turned away from Sandy. 'Go away,' he slurred, nursing his bruised head.

'What happened!' asked Sandy. 'Where's Lauren?'

'They took her,' Frank said simply.

'We've gotta go after them then!' determined Sandy.

Frank shook his head decisively: he wanted no part in this.

Sandy jumped down from Frodo and took Frank's arm. 'I can't track her without you!' she protested. 'Please...'

'You go!' Frank snapped and immediately wished he hadn't. His head seemed about to explode. In a quieter voice he said, 'I'm busy bleeding!'

Sandy pulled him back as he turned to go. She looked beseechingly into his eyes. 'Please, Frank, please...'

'It never ends!' he complained. 'You really think I'm gonna go chasing after that pack of psychos for a dumb blonde?'

'She's not dumb!' Sandy retorted fiercely. 'And she's not a blonde either!'

Frank was slightly taken aback by the forcefulness of Sandy's remark, but he still wasn't going to be swayed. 'Good luck,' he said, and freed himself from Sandy's grip. Before she had the chance to hold him back he had slipped through the front door of the shack, and slammed and locked it shut behind him.

Sandy went over to one of the shack's broken windows and put her head through it. She was desperate enough to put across the situation in terms even Frank would understand. 'Okay – the truth,' she lied. 'Lauren and I pulled a bank job. Those guys were Feds. Lauren buried the money...'

'Spare me,' said Frank, unconvinced.

'What about revenge?' asked Sandy. 'Those guys trashed your house – look at it!'

Frank wasn't worried. 'I'm insured, so don't even try.'

Sandy clenched her fists in rage. 'I am running out of bullshit, Frank!' she cried. 'For Christ's sake, *they're gonna kill her!*'

Frank looked up guiltily. Sandy continued: 'I know it's not your problem... but this person and I – we've been through a lot of disgusting things together ... This person – is a friend.' She looked hopefully into Frank's face, and added simply: 'I don't have many friends ...'

Frank sighed and walked over to the door. He had to face it: he was a sucker for a sob story. He winked encouragingly at Sandy. 'You might not have many friends,' he said, 'but I do ...'

The quiet desert afternoon was suddenly broken by the roar of mighty engines as an army of over forty souped-up customised motorcycles rocketted over the top of the hill and down onto the plains below.

Riding them were a whooping band of Indians, their noble faces alive with the excitement of the chase as they shouted to each other and yelled out their tribal war cry.

In the front, leading them in the pursuit of Michael and Lauren, were Frank and Sandy. Sandy beamed a grateful smile in Frank's direction: these were exactly the type of friends they needed. Boy, would they ever make that louse Michael suffer now!

Chapter Twenty-Eight

Michael had driven Lauren and his two accomplices across the plains and to the foot of the mountain at the edge of the desert. Once there the rough terrain had forced them to travel the rest of the distance on foot, and Lauren had been pushed along forcibly at gunpoint up a mountain trail.

Finally they reached their destination. The view was breathtaking. Millions of years of intense geological activity had created out of the rocks a landscape of wild, undulating beauty. Dotted among the cliffs and weirdly formed rocks stood abandoned adobe cliff top dwellings, their roofs now open to the scorching sun. They stretched back under the lip of a giant, overhanging cave, above which the crumbly jagged limestone mesa rose three hundred feet.

Lauren was led roughly into one of the ruined dwellings and tied to a chair which was propped up against the wall. One of Michael's two colleagues – a fat hairy little man called Boyd – snickered cruelly at the sight of Lauren now so defenceless. With a lascivious leer he reached over to undo the buttons of her shirt. Instantly Lauren brought up her knee, almost fast enough to hit him painfully in the groin.

He backed away just in time and laughed. 'Hoho, she's a mean one, ain't she?'

'Don't you dare touch her again!' snapped Michael and then turned to Lauren. 'I have to apologise for Boyd . . .' he said with almost convincing sincerity.

'What do you want with me, Michael?' asked Lauren evenly.

'Right now?' He sounded surprised. 'I want you to be comfortable.'

Lauren exploded. 'What are you saving me for, you *shit*?'

Michael raised an eyebrow in surprise. This was not the Lauren he had known and seduced all those weeks ago; that Lauren would not have had the nerve to say 'Boo' to a goose. 'You're beginning to sound like the other one,' he sneered.

'The other one?'

'Your friend, the barmaid,' he explained.

'You don't even remember her name,' Lauren said, disgusted at both Sandy and herself for ever having loved him.

'I'm a busy man,' he said callously.

'Well, it's Sandy,' Lauren reminded him. 'And she's not a barmaid - she's an actress.'

Michael laughed dismissively and looked at his watch. It was half past four. Atkins would be flying in soon to make the drop. It was time to get things organised - and put Lauren to some good use at last.

Michael had taken Lauren to the large cave by the cliff dwellings. Boyd and Russell, the other hood, had positioned themselves as lookouts, perched on the roofs of two of the dwellings. Some two hundred feet above them in the sky by the side of the mesa Atkins's helicopter hovered . . . Slowly the leather briefcase was lowered down on a rope.

Michael, protected by the overhang of the cave, looked up in satisfaction. He turned to Lauren: 'You're going to make the exchange,' he told her. He handed her the packet – but not before first removing the vial of Floratoxin.

Lauren looked at him through narrowed, hating eyes. 'I didn't think you'd keep your part of the bargain,' she said distastefully.

Michael chuckled and pushed her with his gun, indicating that she should go out into the open area in front of the cave.

'It's your big moment,' Lauren said sarcastically. 'Don't you want to do this yourself?'

Michael shook his head. 'Atkins is a very good shot . . .' He smiled cruelly and shoved her out into the open.

High above in the helicopter Atkins and Weldon peered down through fieldglasses at the scene below them. As Lauren came out from the cliff overhang Weldon pointed down excitedly.

'Now, do you want to tell me how much you believe them?' asked Atkins as he recognised Lauren.

He drew out his revolver and he leant out of the window of the chopper, taking careful aim. Weldon pulled his arm back. 'Don't shoot!' he cried to his boss. 'She's being coerced – look at her. She's terrified! She's crying!'

Atkins slowly withdrew his revolver and looked back down through his fieldglasses at Lauren. There was no doubt about it: the girl was doing what she had to do very reluctantly.

Sobbing, she reached up for the briefcase which

dangled at the end of the rope and untied it. She cast a glance back at Michael who was hiding in the shadows of the cave, and at the places where she knew Boyd and Russell were keeping watch, and then tied the Floratoxin package onto the rope.

In the helicopter above Weldon pulled it up and with trembling fingers snapped it open.

It was empty. Before he and Atkins had the opportunity to exchange a word, a shot rang out from down below. The helicopter lurched violently to one side, sending the two men crashing into each other.

On the ground Russell raised his gun and fired another shot. This one hit the helicopter's engine; smoke beganto pour furiously from it as it tilted further away from the mesa.

'Do something!' cried Atkins. 'Land!'

'I'm trying to!' rapped Weldon as the helicopter spun sickeningly around.

Chapter Twenty-Nine

Michael looked on dispassionately as the helicopter lurche towards a cliff and, more through luck than Weldon's skill at flying, managed a precarious landing. He had nothing to fear from Atkins for a while: the wide gorge separated them from him. For the moment he had a much more pressing matter to attend to.

He whistled over to Lauren who was standing alone, holding the briefcase. With his gun, he beckoned her to come over to him.

Slowly she approached him. Michael smirked and pointed the gun at her. 'Toss the case over here,' he ordered.

'You'll shoot me . . .' Lauren said quietly.

'I really am sorry,' he said coldly. He moved closer to her and brought the gun up level with her head. Lauren closed her eyes, preparing for death when suddenly Michael let out a yell of pain, and dropped the gun to the floor.

An arrow had pierced his arm. He looked about him in panic as a second arrow hit his other arm, sending the vial of Floratoxin flying to the ground. Lauren dived to the floor, catching it before it could shatter. Michael leapt over her and ran behind an adobe wall as twenty other arrows clattered against it.

Lauren hazily picked herself up, suddenly realising that not only did she now have both the money and the toxin, she was also in a Western. The sound of gunfire as Boyd and Russell began firing at the Indians shocked her to her senses and she took to her heels running for a grove of trees.

All about her, Indians on motorcycles had invaded the entire area. Some of them had dismounted and were sneaking behind the adobe walls searching out Michael, Boyd and Russell.

Lauren finally made the cover of the grove of trees and ran straight into a waiting figure. She screamed involuntarily.

'Aren't you dead yet?'

Lauren heaved an enormous sigh of relief as she recognised Sandy and fell laughing into her arms.

'You came back for me!' she beamed. 'I don't believe it.'

Sandy pointed down to the vial and the briefcase in Lauren's hands. 'Look at you – you made off with the works here!'

Lauren held the briefcase up proudly. 'This is fifty million dollars!'

Sandy laughed and then stopped, struck by an unnerving thought. She remembered what had happened the last time Lauren had been in charge of a case full of money. Gently but firmly she took the briefcase away from Lauren. 'This time, *I'll* carry the money,' she declared authoritatively.

It was Russell's last stand on the roof a cliff dwelling. He was surrounded by Indians who stared at him steely-faced with their bows and arrows ready.

Behind him, Frank climbed up onto the roof and gave him a gentle push. Russell fell, screaming, off the roof and right down into a bed of cactus some ten feet below.

Boyd, on the other hand, had found a place of relative safety in a small fissure which effectively protected him on two sides from the Indians' arrows. Above him at the top of the fissure two Indians appeared. With a knowing smile, they picked up a rock and dropped it into the fissure.

Startled by the sound, Boyd reacted instinctively and fired his gun. The bullets hit the overhang and ricochetted wildly around him until one found its mark and knocked him down dead.

From their vantage point on the cliff across the gorge Atkins and Weldon watched on with bemused interest.

'Are they ours?' Atkins asked his junior.

Weldon shook his head thoughtfully. 'To my knowledge, sir, we don't have a Native American unit . . .' he said seriously. Atkins glared at him and then continued to scan the area. There was no sign of Michael.

From the grove of trees Lauren and Sandy peered out at the battle.

'Serves them right,' said Sandy. 'They never should have messed with us.'

'Yeah,' agreed Lauren. '"Ninja Vixens", that's us . . .'

The girls laughed and then Lauren saw Atkins and Weldon on the cliff top beside their helicopter. She waved at them.

'Maybe we can hitch a ride home with them?' she suggested to Sandy and then shouted after Weldon 'Hey, handsome!'

They moved out into the open to catch Weldon's

attention. As they did so, a figure darted out from the trees and knocked Lauren down to the ground. Without a second's hesitation Sandy raised the briefcase and brought the full weight of fifty million dollars crashing down on Michael's head. He let go of Lauren and lay there, momentarily stunned.

Sandy dragged Lauren to her feet and the women ran off, scrambling up the rocky stone shale at the base of the mesa. Michael quickly came to and started after them.

The girls looked around them.

There was nowhere to go but up. Loose rocks crumbled away at their feet as they slid backwards, desperately trying to find a foothold. Lauren tucked the vial of Floratoxin into her shirt pocket.

Behind them Michael followed on with a murderous glint in his eyes. Like the girls before him he slipped and slided on the loose shale but carried on, possessed by wild-eyed fury.

Lauren and Sandy had by now reached the base of the mesa. Before them stood a large steeply-inclined wall of rock.

'Jesus, am I ever sick of this,' moaned Sandy as she immediately started to look for footholds in the rock and began to climb up the face.

Lauren hesitated and looked on nervously.

'C'mon!' urged Sandy. She was now some four feet up the rock face.

'I'm . . . I'm afraid of heights . . .'

'Oh well, let's just sit here all day with a killer behind us and talk about it! MOVE!'

'I can't . . .' Lauren whimpered.

Michael had caught up with them. Lauren shrank back in horror as he approached her. She looked desperately around for something – anything – she could use to defend herself.

Her eyes slighted on a stray arrow which had imbedded itself in a tree trunk, and she grabbed it joyously, waving it in front of her in a protective arc.

Michael stumbled back on the loose shale, but quickly regained his balance. Throwing his arm in front of his face to protect himself, he once more moved onto Lauren. Up on the mesa Sandy looked down in abject horror; Lauren didn't stand a chance.

Lauren's entire life seemed to flash before her eyes, as Michael made ready to spring on her. Had she spent all those years at drama classes, ballet classes, even fencing classes, just to be killed by her ex-lover somewhere in the middle of nowhere?

Fencing classes!

Lauren went on point and brandished the arrow in front of her like a fencing foil. She stabbed at Michael, parrying his maddened blows, and then thrusting at him and slicing the air like a demented sushi chef. As Michael instinctively backed away from her, Lauren shot viciously out at him. He lost his balance and went sliding back a dozen feet to land flat on his back on the shale.

Lauren rushed back to the base of the mesa and looked up at Sandy who was screaming encouragement. Taking a deep breath and forcing herself to forget her fear of heights, she began to climb up after her.

Growling angrily, Michael picked himself up and stumbled back to the base of the mesa. Lauren and Sandy had managed to reach an outcrop of rock and as he approached they flung a volley of stones at him. He winced in pain as they found their mark and battered his face.

Wilder now than ever and with a trickle of blood

streaming into his eye, he began to climb after them. He had only one thought on his mind – to exact revenge on Lauren and Sandy. The recovery of the toxin and the fifty million dollars, which Sandy was still carrying, were now of secondary importance.

Lauren and Sandy climbed even higher, finding firmer footholds as they reached the more solid rock. They looked nervously down at Michael. He was fast gaining on them, driven by fury and the lust for vengeance. They wouldn't be able to keep their lead on him for much longer.

Lauren glanced over her shoulder at the adjoining outcrop where Atkins and Weldon, who had now been joined by the Weasel, were watching the action agog through pairs of fieldglasses.

'That doesn't look like a collaboration to me, sir,' Weldon remarked tactfully.

Atkins darted a look of pure poison at him.

'What're those guys? On their lunch hour?' asked Sandy, and cried over: 'SHOOT HIM!'

The Weasel raised his telescopic rifle and looked enquiringly over at his chief. 'Which one do I shoot, Mister Atkins?' he asked.

Atkins lowered the Weasel's rifle. 'Nobody,' he said evenly. 'We don't know which of them has got the toxin.'

Nearer the top of the mesa scrubby little bushes grew out of the bluff face. Lauren and Sandy began to grab hold of them, using them to pull themselves further up the incline. Almost as soon as they grabbed them they would come out by the roots, necessitating an immediate grab at a fresh one. But very slowly they were nearing the top of the mesa.

Finally when she was almost at the summit Sandy found and grabbed at a bigger and more securely anchored bush. Beneath her Lauren grabbed hold of the last of the smaller bushes which promptly began to pull itself away from the rock face.

'Sandy!' she squealed.

Handing on with one hand, Sandy reached down to Lauren with the other and found it very much occupied with holding the briefcase of money.

She looked thoughtfully down at the case and then at Lauren's tear-stained and panic-stricken face. With a resigned sigh she tossed the briefcase away. 'There is no God . . .' she said sadly and grabbed out for Lauren with her free hand.

The briefcase plumetted down the mesa face, bouncing from rock to rock until it finally caught the edge of a sharp outcrop. The case sprang open, releasing hundreds of thousand dollar bills which rained down on the Indians who had been watching the scene in the canyon below. Frank looked up in pure, dumbfounded amazement as Sandy's prophecy of him being showered with money was suddenly fulfilled. Then with an eye for the main chance and a healthy disregard for all that the Sixties were supposed to have stood for, he pushed his way into the scrummage to grab as much loot as possible.

With their hearts and lungs ready to burst Lauren and Sandy finally reached the top of the mesa. They dragged themselves wearily to their feet and, with Lauren now in the lead, began to run across the flat mesa top, just as Michael pulled himself over the edge and followed.

Lauren ran on for a few seconds before she realised that Sandy was no longer following close behind her. She stoped and turned around to see Sandy picking herself up from the ground. She had stumbled over a loose stone in best B-movie style, giving Michael the chance to catch up with her.

As Lauren ran back to Sandy's aid, Michael grabbed at the barmaid. Despite a few very well-aimed kicks in the nuts, he managed to keep tight hold of her writhing, fighting body, as he rummaged brutally among her clothes.

'I don't have it!' Sandy screamed in his face. He stopped his search and looked over to Lauren.

'I have it . . .' she said calmly, taking the vial out of her shirt pocket and holding it enticingly before him. 'Let her go . . .' Lauren demanded.

Michael smiled a cruel twisted smile. 'Of course,' he said smoothly and with one powerful thrust pushed Sandy screaming over the side of the mesa.

Her scream reverberated down the canyon as she fell, fell, fell – and landed with an ass-breaking *thud!* on a ledge ten feet below.

At the top of the mesa, Michael advanced on Lauren, who for a moment stood quite still, stunned by what she believed had just been Michael's callous murder of her friend. Shaking herself out of her shock, she turned and looked behind her. There was another drop into the canyon below. But about six feet further out, the mesa rose again in towers of flat-topped rocks, looking for all the world like a gigantic candelabra.

Lauren's jaw set in determination as she decided what she had to do. It was, after all, just like playing stepping stones back at home. The only difference being, of course, that between these stepping stones there was a drop of three hundred feet.

She sprinted for the edge and jumped easily across the six feet divide to the first stepping stone. Michael hesitated, and then ran after her.

Sandy had climbed back up to the mesa edge and as Michael made his jump, she plucked the heavy glass earing off her ear and threw it like a baseball pitcher with all her might at Michael.

It smashed into his head with a sickening thud but he still succeeded in landing on the stepping stone, just as Lauren leapt off it for the next one.

Their acrobtic chase continued as they bounded from stone to stone. On the fourth stone Lauren stumbled, almost loosing her balance, but righted herself just in time to see Michael preparing to make his leap onto her stone.

She looked at the next stone and her heart fell. The final stone was ten feet away. There was no way she could make it unless . . . hell, she thought, what were nine years of ballet training for anyway?

As Michael came over, Lauren gathered up her last reserves of strength and leapt, sailing through the air like a gazelle. Michael immediately bounded after her; there were now only inches between them.

For a moment they were both airborne, and Michael made one last snatch at her – and then Lauren landed on the final stone, completing the most perfectly executed ballet leap of her life.

Michael was a mere two feet short. He cried out in terror and made a final futile grasp for the edge of the stone before he went down screaming into the chasm below.

Michael, reflected Lauren, as she watched him disappear into the distance, was not Baryishnikov . . .

She heaved a sigh of relief as his body hit the bottom of the canyon three hundred feet below, and then raised her head. She could hear applause . . .

Looking across the canyon, she could see Sandy, and Atkins, Weldon and the Weasel. All of them – even the sour-faced Atkins – were jumping up and down with joy and relief. Atkins was cheering and clapping and waving his hands like a first nighter at a Broadway musical.

Lauren blushed, and made a gracious bow. She had to admit it – it had been quite a performance. Just let anyone try and follow that one!

Chapter Thirty

The applause felt good as the rest of the company ushered Lauren and Sandy to the front of the stage as the stars of the show. Lauren was dressed in a black costume and tights with her hair tied tightly behind her head; Sandy wore a long flowing green dress and a wreath of flowers around her neck. They appeared every inch the professional Shakespearian actors as they took their bows to an enthusiastic audience.

They looked, misty-eyed, at the cheering crowd. Weldon and Atkins were there, standing in their seats and showing their heartfelt approval. By their side stood Korzenowksi, a look of pride on his beaming face. Even Frank, dressed like a character from *Miami Vice*, was there, surrounded by a gang of tuxedoed Indians, and with a blonde on each arm.

As the curtain went down on them for the fifth and final time Lauren and Sandy winked at each other. 'We showed 'em, kid, didn't we?' whispered Sandy.

'Yeah...' said Lauren dreamily. 'I never realised acting could be such fun...'

*

Outside at the stage door, Lauren and Sandy, both now changed into chic designer streetwear, found themselves surrounded by a group of admiring autograph hunters and press photographers.

Lauren took her parents, a well-dressed middle-aged couple who had been standing on the sidelines, and steered them into the centre of the circle.

'Mom, this is Mr Atkins, the backer for the show,' Lauren said.

Mrs Ames shook Atkins warmly by the hand. 'I think it was very courageous of you to envision a woman as Hamlet,' she said.

Atkins flushed. 'It was the very least we could do . . .' he harrumphed. He took Lauren by the arm and led her to one side. Taking a thick brown envelope from out of his jacket pocket he handed it to Lauren. 'Your reward . . .' he explained.

Lauren beamed and handed it over in turn to her father. 'There you go!' she said breezily. 'Thirty-five thousand dollars and fifty nine cents – with interest!'

Her parents looked stunned and surprised. Just then Weldon pushed his way through the crowd. He walked up to Lauren and Sandy and shook their hands vigorously. 'What a treat!' he gushed. 'I wept buckets! What an Ophelia you were, Sandy!' And you . . .' He dried up as he looked into Lauren's face; in the glow of the moonlight and flushed with success Lauren looked stunning. Weldon was suddenly completely tongue-tied.

Sandy looked knowingly over at Atkins. 'Uh-oh,' she said. 'The arrow hits!'

'Listen, Lauren,' began Weldon, and found himself staring down at his feet. He looked up. 'Crazy thought, forget it . . .' His voice trailed off.

'Yes, Weldon?' Lauren smiled sweetly at him.

'No, I . . .' he muttered, and then gathered courage. 'I thought you might, um, allow me to take you out somewhere – sometime – no pressure – at your convenience . . .'

'How about now?'

'Now?' he gasped. 'You mean it? . . . Uh, sure, OK . . .'

'As long as Sandy comes too,' she said warmly. Sandy began to protest but Lauren hushed her. 'Oh, now, come on. You can't be alone on your opening night.'

Sandy smiled gratefully at Lauren when a strangely familiar voice behind her said, 'Sandy?'

Sandy turned around to find herself facing a well-built, well-dressed, impossibly handsome man. She gazed appreciatively at him and said, 'I'm sorry?'

'I'm Howie.'

'Howie?' she asked blankly.

Lauren whispered in her ear. 'You remember – "polyester pants, hips" . . .'

'Howie from the phone company!' she screeched. 'My main man!'

Quickly turning back to Lauren she dropped her jaw appreciatively before returning to Howie and smiling her most regal smile. Carefully stripping her voice of its harsh New York accent, she asked in her best *Brideshead Revisited* tones, 'Would you care to join us for a drink?'

Howie smiled and offered her his arm. Like a duchess Sandy graciously accepted it and they started off down the street.

Lauren and Weldon followed and as they made their way Lauren gave Weldon a playful tweak on the ass. He squeaked in surprise but his face betrayed his delight.

Grinning mischievously, they all made their way to *Joe Allen's.*